UNMASKING THE SECRET PRINCE

UNMASKING THE SECRET PRINCE

REBECCA WINTERS

MILLS & BOON

First published in Great Britain 2021
by Mills & Boon, an imprint of HarperCollins*Publishers* Ltd,
1 London Bridge Street, London, SE1 9GF

www.harpercollins.co.uk

HarperCollins*Publishers*
1st Floor, Watermarque Building,
Ringsend Road, Dublin 4, Ireland

Large Print edition 2021

ISBN: 978-0-263-29014-1

07/21

MIX
Paper from
responsible sources
FSC C007454

This book is produced from independently certified FSC™ paper to ensure responsible forest management. For more information visit www.harpercollins.co.uk/green.

Printed and bound in Great Britain
by CPI Group (UK) Ltd, Croydon, CR0 4YY

Dedicated to my four wonderful children,
who've always been my Champions.

PROLOGUE

"ALEX? WE HAVE a new lead. You're to leave for Rome at three. When you get there, take a taxi to the Jupiter Hotel, where you're already booked in. Rigas will come to your room tomorrow morning and fill you in on what we've found out."

Alex smothered a moan. "I can't leave yet, Uncle Zikos." Though he really wasn't his uncle, Alex loved him like one.

"You mean because of Giannina."

"She's my life. I've made plans to spend the weekend with her before she goes back to Greece next week." In an hour he would be picking her up at her apartment.

"I'm sorry, but you'll have to cancel them. This is too important."

Alex closed his eyes tightly, not wanting to hear it though he knew Zikos was right.

But how to say goodbye to Giannina? It was already tearing him apart.

At thirteen, Alex had met eleven-year-old Giannina Angelis the year before his parents, the king and queen of Hellenia, had been killed. Her father had come to Hellenia, an island kingdom in the Aegean near Greece, to discuss shipping business with the king.

She'd run around the palatial estate with him chasing after his dog. They'd laughed and had eaten some treats in the little summerhouse. She'd been more fun than any girl he'd ever met. When she'd had to leave, they'd shared a chaste kiss.

A year later, the men who'd murdered Alex's parents had been hunting for him. Zikos had rescued him from certain death and had taken him to Croatia. He'd fashioned an elaborate disguise for Alex so he could hide in plain sight, and he was given the name Philip Dimas. To this day Giannina didn't know his true identity or that they'd met years ago.

The situation had to stay that way for her safety as well as his. Alex's whole mission in life hinged on finding those monsters and forcing them to pay for their crimes. But until they were captured and arrested, he couldn't settle down and marry the woman he loved.

He shouldn't have allowed his relationship with Giannina to grow at all, but he hadn't been able to help himself. In case the enemy saw through his disguise, it could mean danger or even death to her too. If anything happened to her because of him, he wouldn't be able to bear it.

Alex had been in London for the last month working on a story for the *Daily Courier* as a freelance journalist. It provided cover for what he was really doing here. He could never have dreamed that the young girl he'd met years earlier outside the palace had grown into the breathtaking woman who came to a night lecture sponsored by the newspaper.

She'd approached him after it was over,

telling him she'd even heard him speak at her high school four years earlier in Salonica, Greece. But she'd been too nervous to approach him. Now she was doing an internship at the London School of Journalism. One of her teachers announced a night lecture that featured the noted journalist Philip Dimas and she'd decided to come.

Remembering how delightful she'd been as a girl, he was enamored with her immediately and asked her out for drinks so they could get to know each other better. By the time the evening was over, he realized he'd met the woman for him. His whole world changed that night, and he'd spent every possible free moment with her when he wasn't running down leads.

But he hated it that he couldn't tell her about his mission and reveal his identity. Worse, when the time came that he'd be able to be truthful with her, he had the gut feeling she'd never forgive him for lying to her.

She had to be the most gorgeous woman

he'd ever met. The stunning brunette beauty with her warm, light brown eyes had stood out from every woman he'd ever met. She thrilled him with her native intelligence. Her natural charm and femininity would haunt his dreams until he could claim her for his wife. But he feared that day wouldn't be coming anytime soon.

"Alex? Are you still there?"

"Of course. I'll be on the flight at three." It meant he had to get to the airport at least an hour ahead. That didn't leave him any extra time.

"I'm sorry, Alex. I hope you realize that."

"I do." Zikos was a saint. Alex owed him his life and everything else. "I'll call you from Rome."

After he hung up, he grabbed his suitcase and hurried out of the apartment to his rental car. Giannina would be waiting for him to pick her up. They'd planned a day in the country.

When he reached her apartment building, he rang for her to let him come up.

She'd left her door open. The glorious sight of her in what looked like a new pair of white pants and a lemon ice silk blouse took his breath.

"Philip—" She launched herself into his arms, covering his mouth with her own. Her hunger matched his. For a few minutes he forgot everything else and gave in to his feverish desire for her, clinging to her curvaceous body.

He loved her wavy brown hair that cascaded down her back like liquid chocolate. She'd left it loose and flowing so he could tangle his fingers in it. The scent of her peach shampoo stirred his senses. Everything about her entranced him, but he had to let her go.

"Agapi mou," he murmured, putting her gently away from him. "Something has happened I need to tell you about."

She cupped his face in her hands. "You sound so serious."

"I'm afraid it is. When we first met, I told

you that if another story came up, I would have to take off immediately to cover it."

Pain filled her eyes. "You don't mean now—"

"I'm afraid so. We've been lucky I haven't had to leave before today. I just had a phone call and must get to the airport ASAP."

"Philip—" She moaned his name.

"I wish it weren't true, but I have to investigate a potentially explosive story for the *Forum Chronicle* in Italy and time is of the essence. The last thing I want to do is leave you."

She looked fragmented. "But I hoped you'd fly to Greece with me next week when I returned home. I want you to meet my family. There's so much I want to show you and do wi—"

"I'm sure I would have loved all of it," he broke in, crushing her against him once more. Since meeting her, he'd wanted to take her away and make love to her for weeks on end. But he would never do it without them being married first and the time wasn't right for that. Not yet…

"I can't believe you have to go." She was heartbroken. So was he. Talk about agony. At this point tears gushed down her cheeks. He kissed them away.

"Surely you know I never want to be separated from you. I don't want to go anywhere without you, but I have a job to do. One day I'll explain all the reasons why I have to go alone. Sweetheart, I promise I'll write to you all the time so you won't forget me."

"As if I could." The words came out in choking sobs.

"I love you, Giannina Angelis. One day we'll be together forever. Remember that."

"Philip—" She half sobbed his name. "Don't go—" The pain on her lovely face, the anguish in her voice, was killing him.

"I'll be back. I swear it!" After another long deep kiss, he broke free of her and left the apartment before he couldn't. His only solace was that in tearing himself away, he was removing the danger to her. Alex was glad she'd be going back to Greece, where she'd be safe until he could claim her.

CHAPTER ONE

Three years later,
Salonica/Thessalonika, Greece

"Boss?"

Twenty-six-year-old Giannina Angelis had been drinking coffee at her desk when the managing editor entered the office without warning. She looked up from the latest draft of the financial section of the newspaper she needed to approve. "What is it, Khloe?"

The forty-two-year-old married woman who'd become the managing editor of the Angelis family-owned *Halkidiki News* in Thessolonika, Greece, had never appeared so excited.

"Excuse me for bursting in, but you're going to be astounded when you hear who just called the newspaper. The secretary routed it through to me first. This man is in Salonica and is asking to meet with the editor-in-chief ASAP!"

Giannina had held that position for the last ten months. Prior to her promotion as head of the influential newspaper that covered northern Greece, she'd been the managing editor for a brief period of time.

"Take a deep breath first," Giannina teased.

She rolled her amber eyes. "He's only *the* most famous journalist in Europe, and so handsome from the photographs I've seen, it hurts!"

Gianinna's body lurched. She knew exactly to whom Khloe was referring. In all the world there could be only one man who filled those descriptions hands down, but she let out a disdainful laugh. "Are you telling me that the award-winning, prize-winning, sensational Philip Dimas of all people has actually arrived on *our* Aegean doorstep?"

Khloe's smile broadened. "Yes. I am. I

almost fell over my keyboard when he introduced himself on the phone. He has this fabulous vibrant voice I can still feel."

So could Giannina. Just the thought of the man who'd enslaved Gianinna's heart before draining it dry three years ago caused her to struggle for breath. She sat back in the chair refusing to believe it was true. He hadn't come near her in all that time. "I'm afraid it could be a joke being played on me, Khloe."

"Are you serious?"

Giannina nodded. "Remember my uncle?"

"You mean the guy who blamed you for the fake story he'd had printed in the paper about Prince Alexandros being alive?"

She nodded. "I have every reason to believe he's the one responsible for that phone call."

In her mind Ari had always been repugnant to her, even though he was a member of the Angelis family through his marriage to her aunt. As such, he knew about Philip Dimas, the man Giannina had fallen in love with in London. He'd heard of Philip's abandonment of her. If nothing else, he'd used Philip's name today in the hope of tormenting her.

It *had* to be her cruel uncle Ari Hatzi, a citizen of both Greece and Hellenia, who was trying to hurt her again, this time in an excruciating way. When she'd been an editor working under him while he'd been managing editor, he'd made up a colossal, impossible lie about the missing prince of the island country of Hellenia having been found alive on Mount Athos.

The whole world had had been looking for him, but there'd been no news of the prince since the king and queen had been murdered years earlier. Everyone at that time believed young Prince Alexandros had either been killed secretly or had disappeared never to be seen again. There was no proof he existed anywhere.

Her uncle had attributed the flagrant lie of a headline to Giannina in order to embarrass and ruin her so the board would have her removed or fired. Of course, there was no evidence of wrongdoing on her part, but she knew the reason for his hatred.

She'd made the mistake of criticizing the present dictator of Hellenia in front of her uncle and some other newspaper staff. Her political opinions about the man she called an evil, underworld tyrant had infuriated Ari and he'd rebuked her for it in a humiliating way.

Gianinna's father, Estefen Angelis, was also infuriated, but for a different reason. He'd conducted a thorough investigation of the incident. Not only had he made certain the paper printed a retraction of the lie Ari had perpetrated, her father had fired her uncle and installed *her* as editor-in-chief. He'd also sued Ari for damages to the paper's credibility.

During that period, her aunt Olga started divorce proceedings against Ari, who had disappeared. Gianinna's brother, Nico, had gone looking for him with the Grecian police to arrest him until his trial, but to this day Ari hadn't been found.

"Tell him to come at one this afternoon. We'll soon find out what's going on."

"I'll phone him back right now. This is so exciting if he turns out to be the famous journalist! I can't wait to meet him in person." The starstruck editor wheeled around and left the office, acting like a teenager rather than a mature woman.

Giannina slowly drank the rest of her coffee. She doubted anyone would show up at one o'clock and continued poring over the draft in front of her. To her chagrin, she found herself reading the same copy again and again.

Her mind went back to the year she'd finished her university studies in Paris at the Sorbonne School of Journalism. After graduation she'd done a year's internship at the London School of Journalism. It was there she'd met Philip Dimas. The gorgeous, dark blond, blue-eyed journalist born in Portugal had given a night lecture for the *Daily Courier* and the public had been invited.

Once it was over, she'd approached him and told him she remembered when he'd come to an evening symposium for parents and students at her high school in Greece four years earlier. While they talked, she found herself captivated by everything about him. He asked her to have a drink with him and that was it.

Her whole world changed that night and they spent every spare moment of those four weeks together. She'd fallen so deeply in love with the tall, handsome journalist, and she went into shock when he'd suddenly had to leave for Italy on a story of extreme importance.

Though he hadn't taken her to bed or proposed, he'd told her he was in love with her. After insisting that she was the only woman for him and one day they'd be together forever, she'd assumed he'd meant marriage and that it would be soon.

A week later he'd sent her a postcard from

Rome, telling her he loved and missed her. But there was no return address or mention of meeting up with her or future plans for them to be together. She'd thought, of course, he would ask her to travel to Portugal with him so she could meet his aunt and uncle.

Giannina had learned his mother had died in childbirth, and his father, a military man, had been killed on active duty. That left his father's brother and wife to raise him. She'd longed to meet them and their children, and for Philip to get to know her parents and family, but it never happened.

Over the last three years, she'd received hundreds of postcards from him at her address at the newspaper. He never signed them and simply told her he was on a story. One day he would come for her. On every card he added that he would always love her.

What a fool she'd been to believe him. Devastated to realize his career ambitions were greater than any love he'd had for her, she no longer looked for those postcards. After a few months, she determined to forget him.

Too bad she kept seeing his name in the news for writing prize-winning stories that exposed fraud and corruption in various governments. No one would question he was the best at what he did. The meaningless postcards kept coming, always declaring his love. She'd stopped reading them. His words meant nothing to her.

She took the advice she'd once given her brother about moving on and she started to date other men. Giannina refused to be like Nico, who'd spent his life mourning his first love, whom he believed hadn't loved him after all. Even if in the end a miracle had happened to her brother, *she* didn't believe in them.

Alex left his newly rented apartment on Nikis Avenue and walked through Aristotelous Square in the center of Salonica. A combination of dread because he'd lied to the woman he loved, plus excitement because he was about to see her again, gripped him. He approached the *Halkidiki News* building a block away more nervous than he'd ever been in his life.

After three years separation, he was about to lay eyes on his breathtaking Giannina, who'd enamored him first as a young girl, and later as a woman. It had pained him that he'd met her too soon in London for them to be married. But that wasn't the case now.

The joyous news that General Ruiz and his junta had just been arrested along with one of the two assassins of Alex's parents meant the nightmare haunting him was over. No more threats of danger. Tonight he would be witness to the other killer's arrest. He needed to tell Giannina the news before she heard it from anyone else since it involved her uncle.

That was only part of the reason why he was in Salonica. The other part would be the fulfillment of his dream to marry her. If all went as planned, he would soon sit on the throne of the Aegean island kingdom. And if his prayers were granted, she would agree to be his bride.

But it meant revealing himself as twenty-eight-year-old Prince Alexandros Pisistratus of Hellenia, the young prince she'd once met and played with in the palace grounds. All this time he'd lived a lie and hadn't trusted her with the truth. Philip broke out in a cold sweat knowing it would take a miracle for her to forgive him, let alone be his wife. She wouldn't listen to his reasons. Who would? That's what terrified him.

Through an infallible source he learned that Giannina wasn't seriously involved with another man yet. But he had zero hope she would fall into his arms when they came together in a few minutes. In order for that to happen, he needed time to build her trust again, but he feared it was far too late. He'd broken her heart.

Alex knew all about that devastating feeling. He'd been the walking wounded after having to fly away from her for her own safety. Life had lost its savor since then. It frightened him that if he couldn't win back her love, he'd never be truly happy again.

Because of his love for Giannina, she would have been the one unknown factor who could have prevented him from carrying out his plans to get rid of the dictator who'd taken over his country in the wake of his parents' murders, General Ruiz. Even in his disguise as Philip Dimas, he hadn't dared allowed that to happen. Her safety had meant everything to him.

After his parents' deaths when he was fourteen, Zikos Novak had whisked him away to Dubrovnik. That was the home of the vastly wealthy Novak family on his mother's side dating back three hundred years with an estate and a fortune in oil. Zikos had developed a plan for Alex to win back the throne once the general and his henchmen were captured and arrested.

Alex owed *his* life to Zikos, the man who'd rescued him from Hellenia after the murders. Zikos, also Hellenian, had been chief adviser and best friend to Alex's father. He'd given him the fictitious name Philip Dimas to hide his true identity.

To make the transformation complete, his black hair and brows were dyed dark blond and his black eyes were covered by blue contact lenses. As he grew older, he had to shave every day without fail. So far his disguise had worked perfectly.

While he attended the university in Dubrovnik and became a journalist, Alex never gave up on his quest to avenge his parents' murders and restore the throne to his family. After graduation he left Croatia to establish his journalism career while he surreptitiously hunted down his parents' killers to bring them to justice.

Still on the hunt for the assassins, ten days ago Alex got the surprise of his life through the Hellenian underground. He made the gut-wrenching discovery that Gianinna's uncle Ari Hatzi, of all people on earth, had been identified as one of them. Alex couldn't believe that the woman he adored and had wanted to protect was his enemy's actual niece.

To think that all the time he'd been searching for the killers, her uncle had been a member of Gianinna's family, trying to track down Alex. Hatzi had once been the managing editor of the Halkidiki newspaper. Now he was wanted by the Greek police for blaming a false news story on Giannina, who'd been put in as editor-in-chief.

Alex had read her father's retraction and knew that she and her family had no love for Hatzi. He also knew that when he brought her this news it would be earthshaking. But she was the only person who had the right to know everything before the rest of the world heard about it.

He entered the newspaper office wearing a business suit and was shown to the editor-in-chief's office on the third floor. A charming woman introduced herself as Khloe Paulos, the managing editor, and told him to go on through.

His heart thudded as he walked into Gianinna's impressive private office and found her working at her desk, dressed in a chic tan and white short-sleeved summer suit.

Between her classic features and passionate mouth, plus the mold of her five-foot-seven body, she looked even more exquisite than he'd remembered. She wore her brunette hair in a side part that reached her shoulders. Gone were the long tresses. Those light brown eyes he'd stared into so many times studied him without blinking or warmth. The expression *persona non grata* came to mind as he drew closer.

"Senhor Dimas—" She spoke in the Portuguese accent he'd once taught her and felt gratified she'd remembered. "So it *was* you who phoned. I gave up on seeing you a long time ago. As for those pitiful postcards..."

A groan escaped when he realized how much damage he'd done. Alex had felt searing hurt coming from her and was reeling in pain himself. He sat in one of the chairs placed before her desk. It took all the mental fortitude he possessed not to reach out and beg her forgiveness before explaining anything.

"I didn't know how else to keep reminding you that you were the only woman for me, and still are." If she only knew she was his whole life!

"I lost count a long time ago."

He deserved her contempt and so much more. "Believe it or not, those postcards have always conveyed my love for you, but my life was forced to go in a different direction. I couldn't make the plans with you I'd hoped we could make at the time." He'd promised he'd be back, but she didn't want to hear it now.

Giannina cocked her head. "It doesn't matter, Philip. We've all had our flings, but that time in England was over ages ago. No harm done. Since London you've become even more famous all over Europe. Your accomplishments precede you."

He cleared his throat. "Not without a lot of help."

* * *

"Don't be modest. The latest stories of uncovering the money laundering in France and the failed assassination attempt of the prime minister in Germany have put you and you alone right at the top of your game."

It was clear Giannina had done her research and was pretending their relationship in London belonged to ancient history. But he could see a nerve throbbing in the base of her delectable throat that told him this meeting had disturbed her as much as it did him. Could he dare believe it gave him a modicum of hope?

"If anyone is at the top of their game, it's the brilliant editor-in-chief of the *Halkidiki News*. I knew you'd be exceptional when you took over the reins."

She shook her head, dismissing the compliment. "Why don't you get to the point. Since I know I'm not the reason, what has brought you to Greece?"

More and more he feared he'd truly lost her. This was agony, but it was past time she knew the truth. "My love for you, Giannina," he said forcefully. "But I realize you don't want to hear that because you don't believe it."

"You're right. What's the real reason?"

Unbearable as this was, he needed to go on. "I've come with incredible news. General Ruiz and his junta have just been arrested and Hellenia is now a free country again."

A soft cry of surprise escaped her lips. "I can't believe it."

"It hasn't been leaked to the media yet, and there's more news. I've been investigating a related story, but you're the only person who has the right to it. I'm afraid it has to do with your uncle Ari Hatzi."

At those words, lines marred her beautiful features. "*He's* the latest story you're after?" She sounded angry. "His outrageous antics have already been covered. He was fired for it and has disappeared."

"I'm talking about the unspeakable crime he committed a long time ago."

A frown marred her features. "What else has that despicable man done besides run away before signing the divorce papers my aunt filed?"

"I remember you telling me that you never cared for him, but you didn't want to hurt your aunt by letting her know."

"That's right, but you're talking in riddles. What are you trying to say?"

She sat back in the chair. "I'm waiting for your news on my hateful uncle."

He dreaded telling her the truth about something for which she could never be prepared. It would hurt her, but it had to be said. Tragically, Alex knew she'd never accept comfort from him.

"A few days ago, I learned through my sources in the Hellenian underground that an eyewitness has named Ari Hatzi as one of the two assassins of the king and queen of Hellenia."

CHAPTER TWO

"WHAT DID YOU SAY?"

Giannina's face paled and she looked so stunned, Alex wanted to take her in his arms and never let her go. How would he ever be able to make her understand the reason for his deception and get her to fall in love with him again? Right now he couldn't see a way. The knowledge shattered him.

"It's true. As you said, he's been in hiding. The last sighting of him has led a contingent of loyal Hellenian patriots to Mount Athos, where he's been living and impersonating a monk."

A cry escaped her lips. "You're talking about the Ari Hatzi who married *my* aunt? The uncle who blamed me for a false story printed in the newspaper about the prince of Hellenia being alive on Mount Athos?"

He nodded. "The very one. I'm on my way there now to witness his arrest. It's going to happen tonight."

She stirred in the chair. "What newspaper has sent you on this story?" came the biting question.

Alex shook his head. "No one sent me. I've given up journalism. This is my last story, but only you have the rights to it because I love you, Giannina. You can choose to publish it or not."

"Love?" She mocked the word. "Don't insult me with that excuse." In the next breath she got to her feet and paced the floor for a moment.

He knew this news had rocked her underpinnings, but her rejection of him was killing him. This was so much worse than what he'd imagined.

"Before it becomes public and he's exposed by the world media, no one has more right to know what your uncle has done than you and your family. Even though the assassination of the royal family happened a long time ago, it wounds me that your family will bear some of the scrutiny when the news breaks. I wanted you to be warned and wish to heaven there were a way to protect you from it."

Giannina turned to him, her expression tortured. "My uncle really helped kill them?"

"I'd give anything if it weren't true, but there's irrefutable proof," he murmured.

She let out a moan. "It was a horrible, ghastly tragedy and gave me nightmares for a long time. Our family feared for the prince. No one knew if he was dead or alive." She looked away. "I've wanted to believe he's still living out there somewhere. Unless my uncle did something to him too. I hope he's still alive."

Alex struggled for breath, knowing how badly he was going to pay for this sin of omission.

"Do you know I met the prince when I was eleven? My father took me with him when he had business talks with the king in Hellenia. The prince had a dog and we played together. It was fun."

It was more than fun for Alex. Moved to

the core by what she'd just told him, he said, "You actually remember it?" The subject of the royal family of Hellenia had never come up when they'd been in London. They been so enamored of each other, and it was old news.

"Yes. After the murders, there was news the next day that the prince had been killed too. Some stories said he'd been dragged from his bed in the dead of night and tortured. The possibilities were endless."

He hadn't expected all these thoughts from her. Thanks to Zikos, who'd found Alex asleep and taken him to safety in Croatia with no one aware of what had happened until it was too late to find him.

"I told you about my aunt Olga." Giannina kept talking. "She made a scrapbook devoted to the royal family because Ari was Hellenian. He had to become a Greek citizen in order to marry her. I remember poring over those early newspaper clippings with pictures of the prince," Giannina continued.

"My aunt followed the news that went on in his country. When the tragedy happened, my aunt never got over it or her fear for the welfare of the prince. I'm afraid I didn't either after having met him." She shuddered. "To think my uncle was responsible is incomprehensible to me." Her voice shook.

"I'm afraid your uncle used your aunt for many reasons, including Salonica's close proximity to Hellenia. You're only two hundred miles from Hellenia's capital city of Loria. The country held certain exclusive trade relations with Salonica, including a valuable partnership with your family's shipping line, which General Ruiz tried to maintain without success."

Alex was now in possession of all the details about Gianinna's uncle who'd inveigled himself into the Angelis family.

"Becoming your aunt's husband gave him entrée to one day use your newspaper to support the dictator's ideology. But your uncle was stopped in time. You got in his way and became editor-in-chief. That's why he was cruel to you. For my own satisfaction I want to see that monster arrested."

She turned to him with a pained look. "Are you absolutely certain this man impersonating a monk is *my* uncle? You believe he's living on Mount Athos?" With her guard down for a moment, the Giannina he'd fallen in love with came out, making him desire her more intensely.

"I'm positive. Otherwise I wouldn't be here risking everything to approach you when I know how much you must despise me."

After a pause, "When will you be leaving?"

"Tonight at seven. I've hired a boat."

He heard her sharp intake of breath. "Since you came to me with this story, it's mine to do with as I like. Is that what you said?"

Philip could hear her mind working. "You know I did."

"Then I'm coming with you to see him for myself and take a picture."

His heart leaped. That sounded like his Giannina, who had an adventurous streak. Nothing could have thrilled Alex more. It meant he could be with her for a little longer.

"There's just one problem. If women were allowed to go there, I would have asked you to come with me so we could witness his arrest together."

She smiled. "I'm not worried about the rules forbidding women on Mount Athos. I'll accompany you on your boat as far as the dock at Ouranoupoli, where women *are* allowed. After the arrest is made, can't the police bring him on board? I have a few choice words to say to my uncle."

"You and the Hellenian people. I'll arrange it."

Her bold determination defined the woman Alex was crazy about. She'd get no argument out of him. He walked over to the desk and wrote down his cell phone number on a notepad. After heading for the door, he turned to her.

"If you change your mind, give me a call. Otherwise I'll come by at seven for you."

"I need to talk to my brother first. I may not be able to reach him until later tonight."

"I'm afraid we have to leave at seven so I can be on time for the arrest." By tomorrow she would know the truth of everything. "For what it's worth, Giannina, thank you for seeing me when you have every reason to tell me to go to hell."

His greatest fear now was that she would wish him on the other side of the universe.

Her eyes narrowed. "I did consign you there a long time ago."

"That comes as no surprise to me. If my life hadn't had to go in a different direction and I'd been given my wish, I would have kidnapped you from London and never let you go."

Then why didn't you? Gianinna's soul cried out as she watched his tall, well-honed physique leave her office.

Left witless by Philip's parting words,

she sat down at her desk in a daze. There'd been a time when she wouldn't have let him go without running into his arms first and smothering him with kisses.

When they'd been in London, every moment became a struggle when it came time to say good-night. That month neither of them got enough asleep because it was so hard to disentangle themselves. Just now she'd almost called to him to stay with her. To her surprise, her desire for him hadn't abated. It proved she was close to being out of her mind.

Once he'd gone, Khloe hurried into her office with an enormous smile. "Oh, Giannina—if I were younger and not married..."

She averted her eyes. "You and a million other women, Khloe. Now I need to make a call."

"Of course."

After the door clicked shut, Giannina struggled to get a grip on herself before she phoned Nico. Her pulse raced off the charts. How could she still want and desire Philip?

He'd broken her heart in such a cruel way, she'd thought she was completely over him. Yet she'd just told him she wanted to go with him. It proved he still had a strangle-hold on her heart.

Giannina had never needed her brother's advice more. She hated bothering him when he was the busy CEO of the Angelis Shipping Lines and had become a new daddy a month ago. He and Alexa had named their little boy Nico and they were so crazy about him, she hated to bother him.

But she needed her brilliant sibling to help her make sense of Philip's claim about Ari, let alone his unprecedented visit. She'd never imagined hearing from him again, let alone that he would approach her on anything as shocking as the news he'd brought.

It took a half hour before Nico was able to call her back. "Giannina? What's going on?"

"Forgive me for asking your assistant to track you down. I need advice and you're the only one who can help me."

"You can always call me. You know that. What is it? You sound upset."

She bit her lip. "I'm not sure what I am, Nico. But here's what I know. This morning I had a visit from Philip Dimas." Her brother knew everything about her former relationship with the famous journalist who'd broken her heart.

After a silence, "What's it been? Three years and a ton of postcards with no return address? He actually came to see you?"

"Yes." Her voice shook. She swallowed hard. "When he walked into my office, I'm afraid I had the same reaction as you did after you saw Alexa for the first time in seventeen years."

"He has uncommon courage to face you after what he did. I'll give him that. Has he asked for your forgiveness?"

"No. His reason for coming to my office has shocked me to the core. He brought news no one knows about yet. General Ruiz and the junta have been arrested along with one of the assassins of the king and queen of Hellenia. Philip says Hellenia is now free."

"You're right. I'm shocked and didn't think we'd ever see this day."

"Neither did I. That's the good news. But there's bad news too. You're not going to believe what I have to tell you, Nico."

"Don't keep me in suspense any longer."

"He has information from his Hellenian news sources that our uncle Ari was the other assassin responsible for the deaths of the royal family."

An eerie silence followed. She knew her brother had heard her clearly and was attempting to deal with what she'd just told him.

"No matter how deeply Philip broke my heart, Nico, I do believe his claim must have legs, otherwise he wouldn't have dared face me after all this time."

"It's possible he's speaking the truth," Nico murmured at last. "Ari had a dark side we all suspected. After what he did to you at the paper, somehow the news that he could be a killer doesn't shock me nearly as much."

"He's an awful man, but I didn't think he'd go that far."

"Philip had to be aware of the false news planted in the paper about the prince and blaming you. No doubt he's aware our notorious uncle disappeared once he was fired."

"He knows a lot, Nico. That's why he's so good at what he does. There's more." For the next few minutes she told him of Philip's plan to go to Mount Athos to witness his arrest. "He told me he'd brought the story to me, no one else. Apparently he's no longer a journalist." *He also claimed that he has always loved me,* her heart nagged at her.

"Does he mean for you to publish it?"

"If I want to."

"Along with the capture of the general, it will be the story of the century, but that's up to you."

"I know. I told Philip I wanted to go with him as far as the village dock. I need to know if it's really our uncle. He's going to pick me up at seven."

"Why doesn't that surprise me," her brother muttered.

"You think I'm insane?"

"Of course not. Even if the man hiding on Mount Athos doesn't turn out to be our uncle, it was an honorable thing Philip did to tell you before it became world news."

Giannina had to admit it was honorable. "But there's no question the man has put you in a difficult spot emotionally. You know exactly what I mean, so enough said about the pain he has put you through. When will you be talking to him again?"

"He'll come for me at seven unless I tell him otherwise."

"Then why not go with him and see Ari for yourself. But I caution you to be careful."

She knew what her brother was saying. He worried about her getting hurt again. "I will. Nico? You think Uncle Ari is the killer, don't you? I hear it in your voice."

"I'm afraid so. Now that I think about it, his fury when you criticized the general's ideology explains what was going on inside him."

"I agree." She bit her lip. "Thank you so much, Nico. I love you."

"I love you too. Say nothing to the family yet."

"I won't. Only you. Give little Nico a kiss from me."

After they hung up, her conversation with Philip came back to her. *I'm afraid we have to leave at seven so I can be on time for the arrest.* He was right about acting immediately.

What amazed her was that her brother was willing to give Philip the benefit of the doubt. Nico knew how he'd hurt Giannina by toying with her love for the last three years. Yet he'd given Philip credit for being honorable.

Maybe she was crazy, but a part of her wanted to believe in Philip. What on earth was wrong with her? She couldn't still be in love with him. She just couldn't be! Those heavenly days were long gone.

Alex stood on the balcony of his hotel room that overlooked Salonica. He drank the coffee he'd ordered with an early dinner. Giannina hadn't phoned, but he was still worried that she could change her mind because she didn't trust him. He was a fool to think otherwise.

From the moment he'd entered her office earlier, the urge to crush her in his arms had dominated every moment they'd been together. But for that nerve throbbing in her throat, she'd remained so cool he could hardly believe it was the same Giannina who'd taken over his heart and had never let it go.

After seeing her again, looking more beautiful than he could ever have imagined, he hadn't been able to settle down. Part of the day he'd talked with Zikos, who'd had a *diamoneterion* rushed through.

Alex wouldn't be allowed on Mount Athos without the official permit.

They discussed details of their plan for him to be there when Hatzi was arrested and brought on board. He wanted Giannina there to identify her uncle. She needed to be provided the absolute proof of his identity in order to share the information with her family.

In the late afternoon, he loaded his cabin cruiser with supplies, then returned to his hotel. A group of men loyal to the throne would join him in a second boat. They would dock at Ouranoupoli, the seaside gateway village to the holy mountain.

If Giannina changed her mind, Alex could never blame her for shutting him out of her life forever, not after the cruel way he'd left their relationship hanging. But a part of him was praying her need for truth was greater than her dislike and distrust of him.

Much as he wanted to walk over to her office and intrude on her unannounced, he didn't dare. Once again, he checked his watch. Six thirty. He'd told her time was of the essence. As a newspaper woman, she knew the wisdom in acting fast on a tip. She hadn't phoned him yet. Maybe a miracle was still in store for him.

As he gathered the last few things to take with him, his phone rang. He pulled it out of his pocket and checked the caller ID. Giannina Angelis. Just seeing her name caused his spirits to plunge. He clicked on, dreading to hear she wouldn't be coming with him after all. "Giannina?"

"Philip?" He didn't hear any breathlessness in her voice. "I talked to my brother. He's thankful you're giving our family the chance to know about our uncle before anyone else."

Thank heaven. He let out the breath he'd been holding.

"Just so you know, there'll be a night watchman at the entrance to let you in. He'll show you to the private elevator."

"I'm glad someone's keeping watch over you. I'll be there soon." He hung up, not only elated that her brother had gone along with this plan, but that she hadn't let the pain Alex had caused prevent her from coming with him.

Never had he loved this woman more than he did now. Galvanized into action, he phoned Zikos, who would give the men working for him the signal to meet him at the Salonica dock. They discussed last-minute plans. Alex would join them later that night.

He left the hotel in his rental car and headed for her office, vowing to win her around no matter how long it took, be it weeks, months or, heaven help him, years. Once Hatzi was arrested, Alex would end his deception. Whether she knew it or not, they were in this together now. If she could ever forgive him after she heard the truth, they would never have to be separated again.

The night watchman saw him coming and ushered him inside the lobby to one of the elevators. When he reached the third floor and entered her office, she stood up, still dressed in the same outfit as earlier.

Maybe it was the lighting, but she looked a little flushed. He could hope it was a sign that she was a little excited to see him. If he got closer to her, she'd hear the hammering of his heart.

"I'm ready to leave the office, but we'll have to drop by my apartment for a few things."

"Of course. On the drive over, there's something else you need to know about your uncle."

She stared hard at him. "You speak with such authority, I have a feeling you know a lot more than you've revealed."

"You're a journalist, Giannina. No one understands better than you the need for a great deal of information about a target if you want to cover the news and get the whole truth."

She frowned. "Don't patronize me, Philip."

"That's the last thing I'm trying to do. I

love you. My hope is that you'll start believing in me."

Her eyes looked away. "I want to believe you for the sake of our family and my poor aunt Olga, who has yet to know what's going on."

"It won't be long now. Have you ever been to Ouranoupoli village?"

"Several times with Nico."

"When we get there, maybe you'd prefer to stay at a hotel while you wait for me. Or you can remain on the cruiser while I meet with the men and bring your uncle to you. I can't give you a timeline, but if all goes as I hope, you'll soon be able to meet him face-to-face."

Giannina lifted her head. "That moment can't come soon enough."

"I don't foresee any problems, but in case there are, you'll need to leave your managing editor in charge. There'll be a bedroom for you on the cruiser and food. Pack enough clothes to last a day or two. I have no idea how long this will take. Now's the time to tell me if you've decided not to come with me."

His heart raced in double time while he waited for her answer. "What do you say?" he challenged her. "Are you with me?"

"Yes," Giannina murmured at last. It brought a subtle smile to Philip's compelling mouth, intriguing her.

She grabbed her purse and went down the private elevator with Philip. The confined space meant their arms brushed against each other, arousing her senses. Giannina couldn't believe she was going with him and feared he could feel the rapid beat of her heart.

They left the building and he helped her into the rental car. She gave him directions to her apartment. The interior was redolent of the soap he'd used in the shower. Its scent flooded her with memories of being in his arms while they'd kissed each other, unable to get enough.

"What else haven't you told me about my uncle?"

It took only a few minutes to reach her apartment. He shut off the engine before turning to her with a solemn expression. "After committing the double murders fourteen years ago with the other assassin, Hatzi's mission in life was to hunt for the prince and eliminate him."

Gianinna's gasp over the unexpected news about her uncle's underlying agenda reverberated in the car. "He admitted as much?"

Alex reached for her hand and squeezed it like he used to do to comfort her when she was upset about something. "In truth, your uncle has been leading a double life for years as a recruit of the general. His whole plan was to marry your aunt to get access to the Angelis fortune and influence. Killing the prince was his next priority."

"I just can't believe it."

Alex pulled her to him and kissed her temple. "I know you're sickened by this, but it's better you hear everything from me before the news leaks out."

She was confused by their closeness that felt so wonderful. Yet she was reeling from this latest news and had to find the strength to pull away from him. "I'm glad you told me."

"Come on. Let's go inside."

They took the elevator to her apartment on the fourth floor. She refused to meet those blue eyes burning with emotion. "While I get my suitcase and pack, you're welcome to anything from the fridge. I think there's a cola."

"That sounds good."

Excitement she shouldn't be feeling consumed her to be with him again. While he went to the kitchen, she hurried into her bedroom and threw a few items into a small overnight bag. She also packed her camera to get pictures of her uncle to show the family.

Before she forgot, she called Khloe and put her in charge until her return without telling her the end date or the reason why. Any emergency and she could phone Nico. Then she changed into jeans and a short-sleeved, leaf-green top.

After freshening up in the bathroom, she caught her hair back with a clip and rejoined him in the kitchen, where he was just finishing his soda. She reached for a ham roll and ate it, followed by a cola.

His gaze fused with hers. It played over her, missing nothing, causing her legs to tremble. “You look terrific as always.”

So did he, also dressed in jeans that molded his powerful thighs. She had to suppress an inward moan. The dark blue pullover suited his rock-hard physique. Giannina needed to stop looking at him and washed her hands. “If you’ve grown a few gray hairs in three years, I can’t tell.” Not when he was a dark blond.

He chuckled. “I’ll take that as a compliment.” He reached for her suitcase. “Shall we go?”

“I’m ready.” She fought not to sound too

eager. They left and went down to the car. He stashed her bag in back and started the engine. Before long they reached a dock where a number of boats were moored. How strange it felt to be alone with him again like this, yet not in his arms.

"Have you ever been on Mount Athos, Philip?"

"Yes. One time."

"What was it like for you? My brother went there with our father when he was about ten, but I don't remember what he told me."

"It's a fantastical place with giant monasteries. There are twenty of them built on the slopes of the mountain. A few are found along the coast."

"Do the monks live together?"

"Not all. Some of them isolate themselves in caves called *sketes* and have their food lifted to them in baskets on pulleys."

"You're kidding!"

"When I went there with my uncle a couple of years ago, we slept in a dormitory."

She felt a twinge of pain. *A couple of years ago?* That meant he'd been only seventy kilometers away from her while she'd been working in Salonica.

"How long were you there?"

"Overnight. I found it fascinating. No newspapers."

"No women," she added, putting on a fake smile when her heart was breaking over the knowledge that he hadn't tried to get in touch with her.

"You were close by, Giannina. I would have given anything to see you again, but I was doing an investigation and couldn't risk it at the time."

Of course not. "Did you find what you were looking for?"

"No. But it was good to be with my uncle Zikos. We hadn't been together for a long time."

She heard genuine love in his voice. "I'm sure it was."

They reached the pier and parked. He shut off the engine. "I can see the officers' patrol boats offshore. They're flashing their lights to signal me. The arrest is about to take place. Let's go."

Something was wrong with her. For a moment she'd forgotten why they were here. Being with Philip again had brought back all her old feelings for him that seemed to be stronger than ever.

CHAPTER THREE

ONCE PHILIP HAD grabbed her overnight bag, he held her arm as they walked along to the dock that led to his cruiser. Had he chartered it, or bought it? There was so much she didn't know about him.

As he helped her on board, she felt his touch invade her body, exciting her.

"Are you all right?" he whispered against her cheek.

She could hardly breathe. "Yes."

"I felt you tremble. Don't be frightened. I won't let anything happen to you." He sounded like the old Philip she'd loved so terribly. At that moment it came to her she still did and always would!

"I kn-know that." Her voice faltered.

"Thank heaven you at least believe in me that much."

It was a surprise to her too, but judging from what he'd just said, he sounded as if he'd suffered, as well. She had a hard time realizing that he was here in Greece at last. After three long painful years without him, they were together again, and alone.

No stranger to boats or yachts, she reached for a life jacket and waited for him to untie the ropes. Once she'd sat across from the controls, he jumped on board and slid into the chair to start the engine. His agility had never been more in evidence. She loved everything about him. It felt so right to be with him again. *Philip, Philip.*

Soon they idled out to open water. Gi-annina glanced at the sky. It would be dark by the time they reached their destination an hour away. The warm June night intoxi-cated her, reminding her of nights with him in London when they took long walks and kissed every step of the way. During that time they were together, they couldn't stay out of each other's arms. Since then her life had been a wilderness of pain.

He turned the boat toward Mount Athos and shot her a glance. “You have no idea how many times I’ve dreamed of being with you like this. I’ve missed you more than you will ever know.”

Philip didn’t know the half of it.

Oh, Giannina. Don’t let him get to you. What if he goes away again?

“Those were halcyon days, no question about it. But they couldn’t go on forever and now you’re here for me to witness my uncle’s arrest. Philip, I appreciate your giving me and our family the news about Ari before anyone else knows. It means everything to me that you wanted to protect us. Thank you.”

An odd expression broke out on his handsome features. He leaned over and gently kissed her cheek. It wasn’t the hungry kind of kiss she would have imagined him giving her. There was a subtle change in his mood that made her heart flutter. “I’m thankful that you trusted me enough to come with me." With a sudden acceleration, they moved across the calm sea.

She took a quick breath. "You have an impeccable reputation as a journalist that makes me want to trust you. I have to concede that my uncle is a dreadful creature who should be locked up for good. When I think of what he did and has been trying to do—" Her voice caught.

This time he threaded his fingers through hers and kept hold. His touch sent waves of electricity through her. The old magic was there. In truth it had never gone. She didn't want it to go away but was afraid to trust her feelings for him again in case this was just the rush of the moment for him.

"His power is now over," came Philip's deep voice.

"Wouldn't it be wonderful if the prince is alive and could run Hellenia again?"

Philip pressed her fingers a little harder. "He really is special to you, isn't he?"

Warmth filled her cheeks. "I've thought about that day with him more than once. If he's put on the throne, there won't be another news story to top it."

"I can think of one," he murmured, "but I'll share it with you later."

Giannina couldn't understand what he meant by that. "I'm sure you think me silly for saying that."

"Not at all. I've had certain dreams too. They've all had to do with you. Every time I had to cover a new story, I wanted you with me. I craved to hold and taste you." His throbbing voice sent a shiver through her body. When he talked like that, it hurt too much because she felt the same way.

By now they were approaching Ouranoupoli and he let go of her hand. Mount Athós loomed large.

He slowed them down and pulled into a reserved slip. After shutting off the engine, he stood up. "Stay here for a moment. Two of the priests are coming on board to meet us."

She took off her life jacket as the robed,

bearded priests approached her. Philip made the introductions. "The Angelis family has agreed to let me bring Kyria Angelis with me this far. We'd appreciate your blessing."

"You already have it," the oldest one spoke. Giannina recognized him. His picture had been taken with her *baba* a year ago. "This troubling business has disturbed everyone. We are thankful it's going to be over soon. Give my best to your father, Kyria Angelis."

"He'll be very pleased to know I've met you."

The priest turned to Philip. "We pray all will go well with this arrest."

"That means a great deal to everyone."

"We must not keep you."

Giannina watched them leave the cruiser. Philip rejoined her. "Come below with me and I'll show you around."

"Don't you want me to help you tie up?"

"That other boat following us holds the men coming with me. They'll take care of everything. Rigas, one of the men, will stay here and guard you while I'm gone. I promise you'll be safe."

Her breath caught. "You're leaving already?"

"I have to."

She reached for her overnight bag and went down the steps to the galley. They passed an office. "Use it anytime you like."

"Thank you." She followed him to the end cabin. "The bathroom is between this one and mine. There's plenty of food and drink in the kitchen. Do you have any questions?"

"How long will you be gone?"

"I can't tell you. Hopefully I'll be back soon."

"With my uncle."

"That's the plan," he murmured. "What else would you like to ask me before I go?"

"I've a thousand questions, but they'll have to keep."

"Wish me luck." In the next instant he gave her a brief kiss, this time on the lips, but she wanted much more. Her desire for him was growing out of control. He had to know it before he turned and raced toward the stairway.

With pounding heart, she hurried to the top deck to watch him leave. For three years there'd been nothing between them. Now all of a sudden, the touching and kisses had thrown her off course. She pressed her fingers to her lips. He could have no idea how much she'd suffered after he'd abandoned her. Giannina couldn't bear to go through that kind of pain again, yet here she was, dying for his embrace.

Her eyes tracked his incredible male physique as he joined the group of men on shore. Darkness made it difficult to see their movements, but his dark blond hair stood out. Before long they disappeared.

The tough-looking man named Rigas had planted himself on the dock next to the cruiser. He was dressed like a local fisherman, but Giannina had no doubt he could take care of anything or one if he had to. He nodded to her, making her feel perfectly safe.

For the next two hours she stood at the rear of the cruiser, reliving that month with him. Much of the time he'd taken her for a meal and a drive had followed. They'd park by a lake and reach for each other, trying to make the most of every moment together.

Now things were different because *he* was different. He said he still loved her, but what were his future plans? How long could she count on him to stay in Greece? She was also nervous for what could happen where the arrest was concerned. No matter how carefully he'd planned, he could be in danger if something went wrong.

Beyond the twinkling lights of the village, Philip was out there on the mountain to watch the downfall of her uncle. Her thoughts drifted to her aunt and how she would take the news that her estranged husband was a killer. Better not to think.

It was near midnight before she heaved a sigh and went below to get ready for bed. But when she came out of the bathroom, she changed her mind about sleeping in the cabin. In fact, she didn't think she'd be able to sleep at all.

Still dressed in the same clothes, she reached for her pillow and blanket, then went back on deck. In a minute she'd fashioned a makeshift bed on one of the padded seats. Next, she pulled out her small digital camera and got it set so she could capture pictures the moment Philip returned.

She planned to take pictures of her uncle so her family would have the proof. Those photos would go along with the breaking story she'd been planning out in her mind to publish.

The water lapped against the cruiser, rocking it in a gentle rhythm. A wondrous star-studded sky filled her vision. With the air like velvet, her body ached for the man who'd caused this trembling with that last kiss. She didn't understand him. All she knew was that after tonight she'd never be the same again.

For so long she'd managed to live her life without him. But being with him now had broken down her defenses. This was what Nico had warned her about. Be careful, he'd said. Though she'd tried to harden herself, Philip had this way of infiltrating her heart and body until all she wanted was to be with him.

He'd reentered her world. For how long she didn't know. She was a fool but being with Philip again made her feel alive for the first time in three years. No man was like him. She hadn't been able to get interested in anyone else.

He had that unmatchable power to excite her mind and touch her in a way that ignited her passion. Philip Dimas owned her heart. He should have been wearing a warning sign from the beginning. Caution: to love this man could cause you heartache forever.

At some point Giannina lay back and pulled the blanket over her. She'd set the camera beyond her pillow so she could reach for it at a moment's notice. After a few minutes, she turned on her side facing the dock to get comfortable and closed her eyes. Her thoughts went back to that time in England when Philip had set her on fire. She'd loved him so terribly.

When she came awake later, her pillow was wet, and she heard muffled voices on the dock. She sat up to hear better but couldn't make out words. The next thing she knew a male figure came on board. Her heart throbbed in her throat.

"Philip?" she called out.

"Giannina—what are you doing on deck?"

Her watch registered 5:30 a.m. Relieved he was back, she threw off the blanket and got to her feet. "I couldn't sleep and was waiting for you."

He'd come alone. She watched him slide in the captain's chair and turn on the engine. She sat across from him once more, trying to make out his striking features in the early light.

"What happened? Where's my uncle?"

He grimaced. "We were too late. I'm afraid his friends had already helped him escape in one of those baskets bringing him food. They've made their way to a forested inlet up the coast. That's where we're going and will catch up with him."

Philip had warned her time was of the essence and had to be bitterly disappointed. So was Giannina, for his sake as well as her own.

She knew the inlet he'd talked about. Earlier in her life she'd gone there diving with friends where the water was deep. It was only a few minutes away on the other side of Mount Athos. But unlike the holy mountain, it wasn't forbidden to women. When Philip went ashore this time, she'd be able to go with him and take pictures.

"What can I get you? Coffee? A soda?"

"Water, if you don't mind."

"That sounds good to me too. I'll grab us both a bottle." She went below and retrieved two from the fridge before hurrying back to him. "Here you go."

"You're a lifesaver." He removed the cap to drink. She watched his throat as he emptied the bottle without taking a breath. "That tasted good."

She took the empty bottle from him. "Just so you know, I'm planning to go ashore with you this time and take pictures."

"That's exactly what I want you to do."

His surprising remark robbed her of the fight she'd planned to wage if he told her she had to stay on the cruiser. "What aren't you telling me?"

"Only that you need to stay right next to me when we leave the boat. My job is to protect you to the death, so promise you'll do as I say and ask no questions."

This was a new side of Philip she'd never seen before. His fierceness silenced her.

Mount Athos was silhouetted against a lavender sky. Morning had come to this glorious part of the Aegean with the man at the throttle she'd thought she would never see again. Once they caught up with her uncle, maybe today would be all she'd have of Philip before he left Greece. He'd promised that one day they'd be together forever, but were they just words? She didn't know.

Don't think beyond today, Giannina. Just don't.

During the few minutes it took to reach the inlet, she grabbed the bedding and went below. It was time to freshen up and apply fresh lipstick. Once back on deck, she put the camera in her case and looped it around her neck. Philip's intense gaze swept over her. "Do you have any idea how beautiful you look this early in the morning?"

He sounded so sincere, but a compliment at this late stage only brought back the pain. After this adventure was over, she feared he'd leave her again.

With expertise, he drove the cruiser to the inlet, where several other boats were moored. He shut off the engine and got to his feet. "Let's go," he urged. "I'll help you."

Philip put a strong arm around her waist and lifted her over the side into shallow water like she weighed nothing. She could tell he was in a hurry. He grasped her hand

and together they rushed onto the bit of sand before entering the lush greenery of the forest.

Farther ahead, Rigas waved to them and led the way. Before long they came to a little clearing where she saw six armed men surrounding a pup tent. One of the guards walked over to lift the flap of the tent. With her pulse racing, Giannina pulled the camera out of her case in preparation for the first glimpse of her uncle.

In seconds a scruffy-looking man maybe in his early fifties—hunched over and grizzled—emerged in handcuffs and a blindfold. He wore black-tunic-type clothing like a medieval monk. His silhouette didn't remind her of her uncle, but she hadn't seen his face.

She darted Philip a searching glance, but he was fixated on the man with a frightening expression on his features she'd never seen before. The savage look in his eyes astonished her.

Giannina didn't understand. His set jaw

told her at a glance he was barely holding on to his control. One of the guards removed the blindfold.

"Uncle Ari!" she gasped at the same time she snapped his picture. *It really was her uncle!* The camera slid from her hands and fell to the underbrush.

One of the guards turned to Giannina. "Kyria Angelis? You need to be informed that your uncle Ari Hatzi is arrested for involvement in the murder of the royal family of Hellenia. He's wanted by the Greek police for fleeing arrest, but more importantly by the Hellenian patriots."

She took a step closer to the man who'd been married to her aunt for years, the man who'd caused such pain and trouble for the entire Angelis household. "To think it was you who helped to kill the king and queen."

He'd lowered his head, refusing to talk.

Her rage grew. "All these years you've lived with my aunt, you've had blood on your hands!"

"Don't be so melodramatic."

How many times had he said that to her over the years, disparaging everything she ever said or did. He hated their family and her interference at the newspaper. Talk about sinister…

"And you've been stalking the prince too, all these years!" Her cry rang throughout the forest. She threw her head back and stared at Philip, who picked up her camera so she could put it in her case.

"Let's go, Giannina."

After grasping her hand, he walked her through the forest to the sand. The next thing she knew they'd reached the cruiser. He lowered her to the deck. Once on board, he carried her in his arms and took her below to the bedroom he'd designated for her.

Alex knew this was a traumatic moment for her. It was one thing to have disliked her uncle, but another to learn he was a killer.

He sat down on the end of the bed with her in his arms and rocked her. "Forgive me for putting you through this, Giannina," he murmured into her hair. "But I knew you'd never quite believe this of your uncle until you saw him."

The heaving sobs coming out of her shook him to the deepest regions of his soul. "It's my aunt I'm crying for, Philip." For the next while, all he could do was hold her close and let her give way to her sorrow.

When she grew quiet, he got up with her and laid her out on the bed. Needing her warmth, he slid next to her and pulled her into his arms with her face against his chest. Soon the tears started again, soaking the front of his pullover.

"I always despised him," she spoke at last. "Nico felt the same way. When Ari married my aunt, and my father let them take up residence in the west wing of the villa, a change came over our whole household. Because he came from Hellenia and had no home of his own in Salonica, my parents made him welcome. Baba gave him a job at the newspaper. There's no one kinder than my parents or aunt, who opened their hearts to him."

Alex kissed her forehead. "I'm so sorry this had to happen to your family, Gi-annina."

She lifted wounded, wet brown eyes to look at him. "I could feel his resentment of me and my brother from the moment he moved in. He had a mocking attitude none of us could stand. It still astounds me that my aunt could have fallen in love with him. But she admitted those feelings wore off once they were married."

"Chemistry draws people together, even someone like the man she thought she loved."

"He never loved her!" she cried. "She was the means to an end. I'm glad he's been caught. The worst is over for her now."

At this point, she rose up. "He used to watch me at the newspaper with those icy eyes, wishing I were nowhere around."

He pulled her close once more. "You need

never worry he'll torment you or your family again."

"I'm so thankful he's been caught."

So was Alex. With Hatzi's capture, Alex prayed she would accept him when she learned who he really was. A new nightmare had begun. With reluctance, he let her go and rolled off the bed.

"Why don't you freshen up while I fix us something to eat. We both need food and coffee."

She made a slight nod.

Euphoric over Hatzi's capture, he got busy in the galley to give her privacy. Before long she joined him and sat down at the table.

"I just talked to Nico."

That didn't surprise Alex. She'd once told him her brother was her rock. He believed it. Pleased to see she'd started to recover, he said, "Do you think the news shocked him?"

She stared at him over the rim of her coffee mug. "You mean that Ari's a cold-blooded murderer? No. Nico said he thought Ari was capable of anything. He couldn't be happier to know our uncle has finally met his deserved end. My brother will tell our parents and find a way to inform our aunt."

"That's good. Hatzi will be held in a Greek jail until the Hellenian authorities have him extradited to Loria. Your brother can arrange for him to sign those divorce papers before he's transferred."

"You're right." She took a bite of sandwich. Alex was glad to see she could eat. He'd been afraid she might have been too upset. "Mmm. This is good. I didn't know you were a cordon bleu chef as well as a journalist."

"My lifestyle means I've learned how to stay alive on my own cooking." His gaze studied her features. "I need to fly back to my uncle who has helped me all these years and tell him what's happened. Will you come with me? We'll fly in his private jet. It'll only take a half hour."

Her eyes lit up, thrilling him. "I'd love to

come. But if we have to travel all the way to Lisbon, that'll take much longer tha—"

"My uncle hasn't lived there for a long time," Alex interrupted.

"I don't understand."

No. There was so much she didn't know yet, but soon.

"Uncle Zikos is a very wealthy man with residences in half a dozen countries. We lived in Portugal for a time, but these days he's been staying at his home in Dubrovnik, Croatia, where his family's oil reserves are located. With contacts all over, he'll have heard of the arrest and much more."

She went quiet, but he could hear those wheels turning in her head.

"I'm afraid I've overloaded you with too much information, Giannina."

"Not at all," she murmured. "It's just surprising to learn things about you I never knew before."

"For your safety I wasn't free to tell you everything when we met in London. After today's revelation about Ari, you're my only concern. But maybe you'd rather be with your family and get back to work on the story. We can fly to my uncle's another time."

"Philip—" she blurted, shaking her head. "I'm fine. Honestly. I've always wanted to meet the family that raised you."

"Before we get there, I want to fill you in on my uncle's situation. My aunt died of pneumonia last year."

Another surprising revelation. "I'm sorry. I'd hoped to meet her."

"It's very sad you can't. You would have liked her. As for my two cousins, both are married now with children and live away, so there's only my uncle at home."

"Then he must miss you very much when you're gone."

"That works both ways." He flicked her a glance. "You'll like him a lot. He's been anxious to meet you too, believe me. I don't think he has a single enemy, except for those factions in our world who bring hate and chaos."

"He sounds like my father. Baba's not only well loved, but a fighter for freedom. When he learns the whole truth about what Ari did, I'm sure he won't be surprised. You have no idea how good he was to my uncle, who harbored an obsessive jealousy of him and everything he stood for."

"Some men are beyond redemption and need a miracle to intercede for them."

"He had my angel aunt Olga, but he was too filled with malice to know it."

His blue eyes pled with her. "Let's forget him and enjoy this time together."

"There's nothing I want more."

"Neither do I." Grateful that she didn't hate his guts yet, he got up from the table, admiring her indomitable spirit. "I'll be waiting for you on deck."

CHAPTER FOUR

PHILIP'S INVITATION WAS what Giannina had hoped for three years ago! It had finally happened. She couldn't wait for him to take her on a tour of the city and show her where he'd gone to school. What were his favorite haunts? Was there a certain bistro he loved? A favorite place?

To guard her heart, maybe she shouldn't be going, but she couldn't help herself. She'd never fallen out of love with Philip, and a lot of things about him were starting to make sense. He'd been hiding things from her. Now was her chance to find out what they were so there'd be no secrets between them.

Philip had the backing of a wealthy uncle so he could go where he wanted, when he wanted, in pursuit of a news story. For now, he had an apartment in the posh section of Salonica and had access to this sleek cruiser to get him around.

Dazed by all this, Giannina got busy and did the dishes. Her next task was to gather her overnight bag and camera case. She straightened the bedding on the bed she hadn't slept in and went up on deck.

He'd been watching for her and handed her a life jacket, which she put on. After handing it to her, his hands slid up her arms in the old familiar way. But suddenly he let her go. When he didn't follow through with another kiss, she wandered over to the side of cruiser, having to pretend it hadn't affected her. She wanted him so badly it was torture.

Soon they were speeding past Mount Athos. There was no sign of the other two boats. Though the scenery was magnificent, her gaze fell on Philip, the most attractive man she'd ever met or known. He'd shaved and changed into an open-necked sport shirt. Was it any wonder Khloe had practically fainted at the sight of him back at the office?

Giannina touched fingers to her lips where he'd kissed her earlier. She could still feel the sensation that had swept through her. Yet oddly enough she didn't need to recall her brother's sage advice. He'd warned her this could be a dangerous situation if she allowed Philip to take advantage of her. Yes, he'd invited her to meet his uncle. But what Nico didn't know was that she had no idea what the future held where Philip was concerned.

While they'd been on the bed in the cabin, he'd held and comforted her, nothing more. She'd wanted him to make passionate love to her and didn't know what to make of his behavior. It disturbed her that she still loved him so terribly.

If he'd felt the same way about her three years ago, they'd have been married by now. Though he insisted that he'd always loved her, the fact that he'd never taken her to bed puzzled her more than ever.

Today she'd learned some surprising things about his past where his wealthy uncle was concerned. She suspected she didn't know half of what Philip was all about. Talk about him being an enigma! The only way to get through this situation was to be patient and hope for more. A few brief kisses and touches weren't enough.

She looked out over the water, watching some sailboats in the distance. Truly no more magical place existed than this part of the Aegean. She'd love to go sailing with him. She'd love to do anything with him!

A full sun shone on the blue of the water, a blue almost as beautiful as the color of his eyes. Her gaze darted to him. The sun gilded the dark blond tips of his hair. She should have kept her camera case around her neck so she could take more pictures of him when he wasn't looking.

But that was a foolish thought since she probably wouldn't see him again once she returned to work. She'd promised herself to get rid of those postcards, but they remained stashed away in her dresser at home. It really was past time for her to move on and find a love she could depend on.

Philip would go his secret way. He said he'd given up journalism. To do what? Still, it didn't matter. Better not to have any more remembrances of him. While she was deep in thought, he called to her. "Come and sit near me. I want to hear about your life. We have a lot to catch up on."

Her life? How ironic when she didn't know nearly enough about *his*. But she did his bidding and planted herself on the padded seat. "Since you know I've worked at the newspaper since returning from London, there's very little to tell."

"That's not true," he came right back. "I want to hear how many men at the paper are besotted with you."

She rolled her eyes. "Probably several dozen. But we have a rule about fraternizing with the staff, so my ardent suitors are found elsewhere."

"There must have been someone."

"But nothing serious," she answered honestly. Her love for Philip had ruined her for other men. "Like your work, mine has pretty well consumed me."

"It's possible that one of these days soon you'll be busy publishing an amazing new story."

"You mean besides the story on Ari? A bigger one? The one you *won't* be covering?"

He nodded.

Philip was being mysterious again. Frustrated by his behavior, she shifted in place as they sped through the water. "If you don't mind, I'd rather hear about this huge change you've made that has brought your career as a journalist to an end."

Philip flashed her the kind of smile that had captivated her in the beginning. The man was so incredibly attractive, she looked away. Her intense desire for him frightened her.

"I want a family," came his admission.

"It means I can't be a journalist who travels around Europe at a moment's notice."

"Some reporters do both," Giannina reasoned while reacting to what he'd just said. "There's a married man on my staff who makes it work."

"How often is he in Salonica?"

She bit her lip. "Not as much as he'd like to be, I'm sure."

"That's the point. I intend to stay home and take care of my family."

Giannina had no idea he felt that strongly. "I guess my first question is, where will home be to you? In Croatia near your uncle?"

"No." He sat forward. "I have other plans."

She groaned inwardly. "Does that mean you already know what you want to do for a living?"

Their gazes fused. "I know exactly."

"That sounded final."

"It is. But I'm not certain if the woman I want to marry will be happy with my choice." She sucked in her breath and struggled not to reveal the splintering pain his words had inflicted. He grasped her hand. "Surely you know that woman is *you*. It's *always* been you."

"Please, Philip. Don't joke about anything this serious."

"Were those hundreds of postcards a joke?" he demanded.

"But—"

"I meant what I said on them," he broke in on her. "One day we'd be together forever, *if* it was what you wanted too. Why do you think I want to take you to my uncle's? He's been forced to hear me talk about you for three long years. He's delighted I'm finally free to go after the love of my life."

She really was the love of his life?

"I realize I've waited too long to come for you, though there were life-and-death reasons I couldn't reveal to you at the time. I know you loved me once, but I fear you can't forgive me for staying away this long. Not only that, I have other concerns. You've only known me as a journalist. If we were to get married and I worked in government, you might not like it."

She shook her head in disbelief. "You plan to run for a government office?"

"Not run. It would be a case of being a part of one." He flashed her a glance. "Does that surprise you?"

Giannina was trying to take it all in. "I don't know. What government are you planning to work for?"

"A new one."

New? There he went again, not giving her a full answer. "Somehow I don't see you as a bureaucrat."

A faint smile appeared. "You mean the type concerned with procedural correctness at the expense of people's needs?"

"I didn't say that."

"But you implied it, Giannina."

She cocked her head. "What would you do exactly?"

"Help bring about change to better life as we know it. My work over the years has taken me many places. I've seen and written about things no man should have to witness, let alone live through. Now I've had enough of being a bystander. It's time for me to do something fundamental that could make a difference to people."

"I had no idea you felt so passionately about the news you've covered. I admire you for wanting to promote changes in government when it's so hard to do. For you to want to make a difference excites me."

"But would you be able to handle it being married to me, knowing it will be a full-time job?"

When she'd given up hope, Giannina couldn't believe the day she'd been waiting and praying for had finally come. Had he really proposed to her?

"How can you ask me a question like that? I want you to be happy. If that's the job you want, then I want it for you. Unless, of course, you end up neglecting *me*," she teased.

He didn't lighten up and shook his head.

"I'm afraid that could happen in any marriage, no matter the kind of work or profession. Sometimes it's the wife who's the workaholic and the husband suffers neglect."

Again his comments astonished her. "Do you think I'm that type?"

"I'm not sure."

"Does it worry you?"

"Maybe."

Philip, Philip. "Are you saying I didn't live for you when we were in London? That I didn't try to drag you back when you left my apartment three years ago?"

"That was different. We weren't married."

"Are you saying I didn't chase after you like some of the women in the audience once you'd given that lecture?"

"You weren't like that."

"I was exactly like that, but I wanted you and didn't dare act like the others in case it turned you off."

"It worked, Giannina," he murmured, but there was no smile. The knowledge that he'd just proposed marriage to her in the most unorthodox way she could have imagined had stunned her beyond belief.

"What are you thinking, Philip? From what I understand, most husbands don't want a wife who clings to them constantly. Though there are some married couples who work together, I think it would have its own problems."

"I'm sure you're right." He started to slow down the boat. They'd reached the pier in Salonica. Before she knew it, he'd glided the cruiser into the slip with expertise. Rigas waved to them, having come in on the other boat. The police must have brought her uncle on their boat, but she didn't see it. Philip shut off the engine.

"Giannina?" He'd turned to her. "Do you still love me? Can you forgive me for staying away so long?"

The question caught her totally off guard. "How can you ask me that when you *know* you're my whole life!" she cried. "Why am I here now if I haven't forgiven you? No sooner did you come to my office than I told you I wanted to go with you on your boat. Ari had nothing to do with my leaping at the chance to be with you again. If that doesn't tell you everything you want to know…"

He cupped the back of her neck and gave her a kiss to die for. When he let her go, he said, "I'm afraid there's much more I need to tell you about me. It could affect the way you feel."

"Then tell me now," she begged him.

"I'd rather wait until we reach Croatia, where we'll have total privacy. Will you trust me putting you off just a little longer?"

She pressed an urgent kiss to his lips the way she used to do. "I guess I'm going to have to. Don't keep me waiting too long."

"I swear I won't."

They both got to their feet. She removed the life jacket and put it on the banquette. After grabbing her overnight bag, he cupped her elbow and they stepped onto the dock. While Rigas tied things up, they left for the parking area and got in Philip's car. He put her bag in the back seat and they were off.

"What's going on in that fascinating mind of yours that has made you go quiet?" They were headed for the airport.

"Maybe it's because you've just asked me to marry you."

He grasped her hand. "I wanted to ask you in London."

"Every night we were together I hoped you would propose," she admitted.

"I ached to. Don't you know I love you with every fiber of my being, Giannina?"

"Philip." She half moaned his name. "I feel the same way."

They drove to the small airport where his uncle's private jet stood on the tarmac. It was hard to believe she was finally going to meet the uncle who'd taken care of him once he'd lost his parents.

A steward greeted Giannina as she and Philip climbed inside the luxurious jet. He showed them to the club section, where she sat across from Philip. The fasten-seat-belts sign went on and the private jet taxied to the runway.

He darted her a glance. "Have you phoned your brother to let him know what's going on?"

"I will when we arrive."

"We should be there in thirty minutes. I don't want him to think I've kidnapped you like I wanted to do back in London."

"Can you at least tell me what stopped you from spiriting me away back then, Philip? Please don't tell me it was because you had to cover a story by yourself and couldn't bring me along."

"The truth is I didn't want to put you in dangerous situations. I couldn't let anything happen to you."

"Are you saying your life was in danger covering those stories?"

"Even in London my life was in constant danger." His admission sobered her. "But there was another reason too. You'd just finished your formal schooling and needed to get back home to work on your family's paper. Because of your hard work, you're now editor-in-chief of one of Europe's most widely circulated newspapers. The numbers are growing. Have I told you how proud I am of what you've accomplished already?"

They'd reached cruising speed and the seat belt light went off. "Even if my father owns it?"

"Maybe more so. He would never make you the head if he didn't know his daughter would turn it into a total success. Do you love it?"

She shot him an amused glance. "You mean the way you love being the top celebrated journalist in Europe?"

"Have I ever said I did?"

His question threw her. She leaned forward. "I just assumed as much. Are you saying you don't?"

He quirked one eyebrow. "It has provided me with a living."

"Plus adventures and literary prizes envied by your peers," she added.

"I've been fortunate, but there are other ways to earn my daily bread that I believe will bring me more satisfaction."

He'd told her that his life as a journalist was over, but it still surprised her. "After the life you've led, what will you do to make up for all the adventure you've known?"

"Many things I've longed to tackle for years. But for now I want to know the answer to the question I asked you a few minutes ago. Since you've run the *Halkidiki News* for a while, do you find that you love it?"

No one had ever asked her such a probing question. She had to think about it while the steward served them coffee. "I wouldn't say I love it, but I can't think of anything else that would stimulate me as much. At an early age, I loved reading the paper. Now that I'm in charge of putting one out every day, there's a certain satisfaction in knowing it serves the public in a way nothing else does."

"That answer explains why you captivated me from the beginning. Among everything else, you have an intriguing mind and a vision for what's important."

"Hardly." She might love his compliments, but she wanted to hear what else he had to tell her. "I can't put out a good newspaper without good reporting. A journalist like you only comes along once in several decades. Now that you've given up your career to do something else, the media is going to mourn the loss."

"You flatter me, Giannina." He got to his feet and returned their coffee cups to the sideboard just as the fasten-seat-belt sign flashed on. "We're almost there. Buckle up."

"I bet you can't wait to see your uncle."

"You're right." That sounded definite. For so long she'd wanted to meet him and learn more about Philip's past. During the time they'd been in London, she'd fallen madly in love. But she hadn't known all of him because he'd held a great deal back from her.

Since he'd come to her office in Salonica,

she'd seen sides of him he'd never revealed. Much of his life had been a secret to her. There was more to this man than she would ever have dreamed, including the fact that he'd suddenly given up a sensational career. Too many thoughts bombarded her. But the fact that he'd asked her to marry him would have to satisfy her until she heard the rest.

She kept looking out the window, willing herself to be patient until he was ready to tell her everything. Before long the walled city of sixteenth-century Dubrovnik rose up to meet them. The blue waters of the Adriatic on the Dalmatian Coast dazzled the eye as they drew closer.

After landing, they left the jet and he carried her bag to a black, elegant sedan waiting for them. The delightful temperature had to be in the midseventies. She saw the driver nod to Philip, who smiled at him. This had been his world and she hadn't known a thing about it. He'd kept so much from her and she had to admit it hurt.

Philip got in behind her and closed the

door, placing her bag opposite them. After they fastened their seat belts, he spoke Croatian to their driver, Ivan, then turned to her. "I told him to take us directly to Cavtat."

"Is that a suburb?"

"Not exactly. It's the little town where my uncle lives about five minutes from here. His villa on the mountain is surrounded by pines and forests of cypress trees. If we have time, I'll take you to explore Dubrovnik. It all depends on what he has planned for us."

Her eyes fastened hungrily on the landscape that had been deemed a UNESCO world heritage site. "This is the stuff dreams are made of. It's like looking at pictures in a fairy tale. I feel like I'm living in it with you."

He gripped her hand and squeezed it. They followed the tree-lined road near the shore, then climbed into the green vegetation. With the sea below, she couldn't imagine a more picturesque setting. As the car wound around, Giannina let out a cry. Somehow, she hadn't been prepared for what she saw amid the greenery. This was no villa. He'd brought her to a Gothic palace so spectacular, she was close to speechless.

"Philip—when you talked about your uncle, I had no idea."

"The family on his mother's side dates back many centuries."

"It's glorious."

"So is the estate. We'll go down to the stable later and see it on horseback. When we were in London and went riding on Wimbledon Common, I could see what an accomplished rider you were. I've looked forward to the day when I could bring you here. Come on. Let's go in. Uncle Zikos is waiting for us."

He released her hand, then opened the door and got out before helping her. In the periphery she watched a man emerge from the palace.

"Marko," Philip greeted him.

The other man smiled, then reached for

her bag while Giannina was ushered inside and up a picture-lined stairway to an ornate salon on the second floor.

They'd barely entered the double doors when a distinguished-looking man who appeared to be in his midsixties hurried toward them. Silver streaked his dark hair. He was of average height and had penetrating brown eyes. She saw no resemblance between him and Philip. Either Philip's mother or father had bequeathed him his dark blond coloring and blue eyes.

Judging by his uncle's casual clothes and boots, she imagined he did a lot of riding too. His fit physique indicated he was an active man, and she had to admit he had a presence.

She watched through teary eyes as they embraced, admiring this man for raising his brother's son who'd lost his family at such a vulnerable age.

"Uncle Zikos Novak?" Alex spoke in Greek. "May I present Giannina Angelis, the editor-in-chief of the *Halkidiki News*, and the daughter of the famous shipping owner Estefen Angelis."

Zikos released him and reached for Gianinna's hand. "It's a great privilege to meet you at last. Philip has talked of nothing but you since he met you in London." He kissed the back of it.

"I could say the same thing about you. He told me about the time you and he traveled to Mount Athos. He said it was an amazing experience living with the monks, but more amazing being with you."

A smile wreathed his face. "We've had many wonderful adventures together. Unlike my son, Baldo, Philip has a desire to explore life to the fullest. I'm convinced it's what has made him an exceptional journalist. You've heard about people whose minds soak up knowledge like a sponge and act on it. That's Philip. He can't get enough. I have trouble keeping up with him."

"That doesn't surprise me," she murmured. "When I met Philip, he had already gained a sterling reputation as a top journalist. I found him a fascinating lecturer."

"Tomorrow morning I'll let you look at an album of pictures of him growing up with my family. There are photos of his college graduation, but right now I imagine you're tired after the ordeal of your uncle's arrest. You and Philip need to enjoy yourselves for what's left of the rest of the day and evening. Marko will show you to your room, where I've arranged for your dinner to be served."

"I can't thank you enough, Kyrie Novak."

"Call me Zikos. We don't stand on ceremony around here."

She nodded.

"I'll come to your suite in a few minutes," Alex whispered and watched her leave the salon with Marko.

After the door closed, Zikos smiled. "She's a lovely woman. Though I'd seen pictures of her in the newspaper and the photos you showed me, none of them do justice to her in the flesh. How is she bearing up?"

His jaw hardened. "Amazingly well considering what she just learned about Hatzi."

In a low voice Zikos asked, "How much does she know about *you*?"

"Very little. Today I asked her to marry me. Before the night is over, she'll know everything."

"You've waited a long time for this day."

Alex nodded. "She still believes you're my blood uncle. In all honesty, I feel that you are." Emotion poured out of him. He hugged his uncle for a long time. "Remember that I'm naming you my prime minister." Alex drove the point home. "I hope we're clear about that. Father was about to make you his own prime minister until that ghastly night."

Zikos's eyes dimmed for a moment. Clearing his throat, he said, "You and I will convene the old parliament that's ready to serve you. Before long there'll be a coronation. It can't come soon enough for every Hellenian."

Alec swallowed hard. "I couldn't have

done anything without you. No man ever had a better friend than you. I owe you my life, Zikos."

"Your father saved mine years ago from a bullet during the war. If he hadn't given me help on the battlefield, I would have died. We became great friends and stood up for each other at our weddings. It was my privilege to take you to safety when General Ruiz swept in. But his days are over."

"After all this time…"

"That's right. Judging by the way you feel about Giannina, I'd say it should have come yesterday."

"Even though I've proposed to her, it's more than possible she'll refuse me when I reveal who I really am. I've known fear, but nothing like I'm experiencing now. I may have lost her for good, Uncle."

"Nonsense. When she learns your reasons for protecting her, I feel certain she'll understand."

He shook his head. "If I don't miss my guess, trust means everything to Giannina.

Ari broke her family's trust. I have to admit I'm frightened when she hears that I've broken hers for three long years."

"Have faith, my boy. Your reasons aren't like anyone else's. I'll be in my office in case you need me. Go and enjoy this precious time with her."

Philip gave him another hug and left the salon, breathless to spend time with Giannina. She could have no idea how he'd longed to be rid of the pretense and emerge as his total self. But as he knocked on the door of her suite, fear swept through him again. In London she'd fallen for a journalist named Philip Dimas with dark blond hair and blue eyes. She'd loved him, but she might not like Prince Alexandros, an unknown in every way.

He thought about how he'd feel if their positions were reversed. If she were the one in disguise, she would be breathtaking whether she were a blonde or a redhead with green or blue eyes instead of warm brown. In his gut he knew the transformation wouldn't matter to him, but he couldn't speak for her.

"Come in."

Alex walked in the sitting room. The smell of her shampoo preceded her appearing in a pair of tan pants and a café-au-lait print blouse. When he'd first met her, he'd thought her a miracle of femininity and curves.

She'd left her wavy brunette hair loose to let it dry. Never had she looked more enticing to him than she did right now. "Do you have everything you need?"

Her smile melted him. "Your uncle is very kind. I'm being treated like a queen."

"He knows how much I love you. Just now I told him I asked you to marry me. He heaved an enormous sigh of relief."

She threw her arms around his neck. "So did I."

He laughed. They clung to each other and kissed until they couldn't breathe. With reluctance he relinquished her lips. "Let's eat and take a ride before it gets too dark.

When we get back, we'll have that long talk I promised you."

She pressed her lips to his jaw before they walked over to a small dining table where their meal had been placed. He pulled out a chair, touching her hair intentionally as she sat down. It was like pure silk. The need to twine his fingers in it left him with unassuaged longings that were growing out of control.

"My uncle has had a favorite Croatian meal prepared in your honor."

"That's exciting. What's it called?"

"Black risotto because of the squid ink. Since I know you like fish, I think you'll enjoy this. I'll warn you now the seafood flavor is intense. It's made with squid, olive oil, red wine and garlic."

"Squid, huh?" Her soft brown eyes twinkled in amusement.

He watched her take a bite and grinned. "What's the verdict?"

She munched for a minute. "I think it

will be an acquired taste, but don't tell your uncle I said that."

Philip chuckled.

Once they'd finished eating apple-cherry strudel, another Croatian delicacy, they left her suite. He walked her down a rear staircase and out the back of the palace. Their arms and hips brushed against each other as they headed for the stables in the distance. Desire licked through him.

"I haven't ridden for ages," Giannina chatted. "I've been too busy at the paper."

"There hasn't been a lot of time for me either. I've chosen a chestnut mare for you named Yasmine. Rolf has everything ready for us. The older man has been in Zikos's employ at least twenty years."

"Then you know him well. How lovely, Philip."

"His loyalty means everything."

She nodded. "Do you have a favorite horse here?"

"Yes. Haj, an Arabian I'm particularly fond of. There he is now."

Rolf had brought their mounts out in the open. Haj neighed when he saw Alex coming.

Giannina had ridden from childhood and walked around to get acquainted with Yasmine. "You're a beauty." The mare nudged her. "Shall we go for a ride?" She took the reins from Rolf and swung herself in the saddle with feminine grace.

Alex mounted his black gelding. "Ready?" Giannina was the beauty he'd loved for so long.

They rode side by side along one of his favorite trails through a grassy meadow of wildflowers. It rose higher and higher. He felt they'd entered another world and needed to treasure this moment before his revelation ruined everything.

CHAPTER FIVE

A WARM BREEZE ruffled Gianinna's hair. When they reached the summit, her eyes took in the small town at the base of the mountain where the land met the sea. The sun had dropped into the ocean, providing a magnificent backdrop for Philip silhouetted astride Haj.

His chiseled jaw and features stood out. No man alive could ever match his sinfully good looks. He had a virile masculinity unique among the men she'd met. But the outward appearance was only a portion of what made him the man Giannina loved. A fire burned inside him combined with intelligence and a certain elegance that set him apart. His instincts, his drive, fascinated her. To think he was going to be her husband!

Giannina knew he'd given up journalism for something else far more challenging to him. That's what he still had to tell her. She couldn't imagine what it was but realized he could do anything if it was what he wanted. Not every man or woman had that remarkable ability. He'd laid claim to her heart a long time ago and she adored him.

"Do we really have to wait for that talk?" She smiled at him. "I'd hoped during this lovely ride you would open up to me. We're alone at last. You do realize that when you left me in London, you promised that one day you'd disclose all the reasons for your behavior over the last three years. On the boat earlier you said the same thing. Yet here we are and I'm still in the dark."

A troubled look had crossed over his handsome features. "You're right. It's time." There was a solemnity about him that surprised her. "But I'd rather talk to you in your apartment. Let's go."

He'd asked her to give him time. Her heart

beat faster in anticipation of what he would tell her. *Just a little longer, Giannina.*

When they reached the stable, she quickly dismounted and handed the reins to Rolf. "Yasmine is a treasure."

"Philip chose her especially for you."

She smiled at the older man, then at Philip. "He has a good eye."

"Indeed he does."

Philip jumped down and accompanied her to the palace. They walked up the back stairs to her suite. When they reached the door, she thought he'd come right in with her. But she'd been wrong.

"Forgive me, Giannina, but I need to freshen up and will join you in a half hour."

"I don't understand. Do you need to talk to your uncle again?"

"No, but what I have to do first is important."

What was going on with him? "How about another kiss before you go."

"There's nothing I want more." He caught

her in his arms and gave her a long hungry kiss that wasn't nearly enough.

"Promise you won't leave me like you did three years ago and never come back?"

"I swear I won't be long."

"I'll be waiting for you," she said, struggling not to show her disappointment. "Thank you for the fabulous ride."

His dazzling blue gaze took in every feature. It took everything not to throw her arms around him again.

"Remember how much I love you."

Why would he have said that to her? His parting words filled her with a strange foreboding. What should be the happiest night of her life was turning into something else she couldn't comprehend.

Alex took off for his apartment down the hall. He had everything he needed to transform himself and hurried in the bathroom. After fourteen years he was finally going to be rid of his disguise.

First, he removed his shirt and took out

his blue contact lenses. With that accomplished he reached for the permanent black dye. Once he'd put on gloves, he brushed it into his dyed blond hair, saturating it.

During the wait while the black color penetrated to turn his hair back to its original color, he dyed his blond eyebrows black. Then he stepped in the shower to shampoo his hair and brows. He stared in relief as the black residue drained away. Once he'd stepped out, he removed the gloves and reached for a towel to dry his face and hair.

The test came when he looked in the mirror a few minutes later to see the result.

"You're a new man, Alex. The man you're supposed to be. Your enemies won't know you. Neither will Giannina."

Feeling sick to the pit of his stomach as he imagined her reaction, he went in the bedroom and pulled a white linen shirt from the closet. Combined with a pair of stone-gray pants, he finished getting dressed and rolled the sleeves to the elbows. He slipped on well-worn brown leather sandals, ready to meet his fate. This could be the beginning of the end of his dreams if she couldn't forgive him. But it was too late to back out now.

Tonight she'd admitted that she loved him. Her response to his kisses was everything he'd been praying for. But knowing what was coming had brought his deepest fears to the surface—fears that had been plaguing him from the beginning.

Giannina was a brilliant woman in her own right, the head of a renowned newspaper because she deserved to be the editor-in-chief. She was desirable beyond belief. While they'd been apart, it was a miracle she hadn't fallen in love and married another man.

Alex had prayed she'd wait for him, no matter how long it took. Even though she'd admitted on the cruiser that she still loved him, he knew the damage he'd caused. Could she overcome the revelation he still had to tell her?

Though he'd asked her to marry him,

there were no plans to make until she'd learned the whole truth about him. He needed to give her all the reasons why it had been necessary to deceive her. But in his gut he knew what was going to happen. The mere thought of her reaction shook him to the core of his being.

With no time to lose, he headed for her apartment.

After freshening up, Giannina waited for Philip on the love seat. She'd texted Nico to let him know about the arrest and that she was in Croatia. But she didn't reveal anything personal about her and Philip yet. That could come later, after their talk.

She'd just finished sending it when she heard a knock on the door. "Come in, Philip."

Giannina looked up expecting to see him walk in the sitting room. Instead, a tall, black-haired stranger stood at the entrance—a drop-dead gorgeous male defying ordinary description. Her breath caught.

Beneath black brows his eyes gleamed like black fires. The phone slipped from her hands. Though at first glance she didn't know who he was, there was something hauntingly familiar about him.

"Giannina?" The deep voice sounded like Philip's, penetrating to her insides. She didn't understand what was happening and started to tremble. "I'm sorry if I alarmed you," he murmured. "You've known me as Philip Dimas for one reason only. I feared you'd be made a target by my family's enemies and I couldn't allow that to happen. Since London I've wanted to introduce myself.

"My real name is Alexandros Cimon Pisistratus. Just so you know, before I was taken to safety, everyone called me Alex. It's the name I told you to call me when we played together in the palace grounds years ago."

If ever Giannina had been the type of person to faint dead away, this would have been the time. Fortunately, she was still seated.

He came inside and shut the doors. Dressed in gray pants and a white shirt open at the throat with sleeves rolled to the elbow, he possessed the raw, sensuous masculine appeal of Philip. But his black hair and eyes brought out another element that turned him into an entirely different person from the one who'd stolen her heart three years ago.

This man appeared bigger than life, possessing a magnetic aura that shouted he was the missing prince of Hellenia. He stood across from her with his hands on his hips in a totally male stance that made him unforgettable. His gaze burned into hers.

While in a stupor over what was happening, her mind recalled the young, black-haired prince she'd met years ago. Even then she'd seen the promise of the magnificent man in the good-looking thirteen-year-old. After having disappeared for years, here he was in the flesh! It couldn't be… It just couldn't!

He didn't say a word while she tried to fathom one pertinent fact. *There was no Philip Dimas!*

All this time he'd been the prince in disguise while the world wondered if he'd died. The spectacular journalist the world had acknowledged and feted for the years following an early college education had never existed. Their relationship had never been real.

Everything had been a *lie*!

As she started to come back to life after being frozen in place, pain such as she'd never known attacked her entire body. It started in her heart and radiated to every extremity, causing her to cry out in agony.

She shot to her feet, incapable of thought except one. "Welcome to the world you were born to, Your Highness. It's now clear that *this* is the story you've been alluding to, the one that puts the arrests of my uncle and the general in the background. Call my managing editor. She'll arrange for an interview with you when you're ready to announce your return to the throne."

The whiteness of Gianinna's face would stay with Alex for as long as he lived. Everything he'd feared and more had come to fruition with nightmarish clarity.

His heart came close to failing him as she dashed into the bedroom. He reached the entry to her room before she could slam the door in his face.

The plight of Odysseus upon coming home from the Trojan War filled his mind. After ten years absence as prince of Ithaca, Odysseus yearned to be with his faithful, beloved wife, Penelope, and returned dressed as a wily beggar she didn't recognize. Yet once he revealed himself to her, she remained cautious, wary of being hurt and deceived. In the end she set him a test that only the true Odysseus could pass.

Alex couldn't help but wonder what test Giannina would set for him so he could regain the love she'd once felt for Philip.

Tragically the two men were not the same in her eyes. He would have to win her heart and soul as Alex, but he might not have the luck of Odysseus and lose his reason for being.

She sank down on the side of the bed with her face buried in her hands.

"Giannina?"

She slowly looked up. A light had gone out of her eyes, causing a physical change in her countenance. He'd accomplished the perfect deception, but the revealed truth had done a kind of damage from which they might never recover.

"We have to talk."

"I wanted to talk during our horseback ride," she responded with amazing calm. "Since the moment we met in London, I wanted to tell you that that I'd hoped you would ask me to be your wife. But I was dying to be the wife of Philip Dimas."

He cringed inwardly while he waited for the rest.

"Now I know why you put me off so long.

Your transformation has said it all. I appreciate the trouble you went to so I could be there for Ari's arrest and know the truth. He stole your life away from you, and your uncle gave you a new one. Please give that remarkable man my regards and thank him for his hospitality. I'm happy for both of you. Now I'd like you to leave me alone."

Alex couldn't do that until he'd told her everything. "I'll tell him, but you need to know that Zikos isn't my uncle."

She gave a despairing shake of her head. "Of course he isn't. I kept looking for a family resemblance but couldn't find one."

Her words cut him to the marrow. "He was my father's right-hand man and would have been made prime minister but for the assassination."

Anger shot her cheeks with color. "Next I suppose the home in Portugal and all his residences around the world were sheer fabrication on your part. Small wonder you never took me there to meet him."

He swallowed hard. "Zikos is a Hellenian citizen who'd fought in an earlier war alongside my father when they were young men. He lived in Loria, where he met his wife. In time he became the chief assistant to my father. That happened after my grandfather, the former king, died of pneumonia and my father was crowned king.

"The night my parents were murdered, Zikos brought me here to his mother's family home, where we've been safe from the enemy. He has treated me like a son."

She averted her eyes. "He's a true hero for what he's done, but I've heard enough."

"You haven't heard everything yet."

Giannina hugged her arms to her waist. "Seeing you like this is enough. It's all making sense now. I was amazed you kept dating me after that first night when we had drinks."

Where was she going with this? "What do you mean?"

"You did your research all right. Ari Hatzi was your target and once we started seeing each other, you discovered I was his niece. There was no stopping you because I'd fallen head over heels in love with you. You saw the perfect way to learn more about one of the men you'd been tracking secretly. His relationship with my family was like finding gold, wasn't it?"

His jaw tautened. "You couldn't be more wrong. I only knew his name *after* you told me about him and how mean he'd been to you growing up. But I didn't learn until ten days ago that he'd helped kill my parents."

"You mean it was just a coincidence," she mocked with cutting scorn.

"Yes. An incredible coincidence. You only have to talk to the eyewitness who came forward ten days ago to know I'm telling the truth."

"What naive little fool do you take me for? I couldn't believe you were attracted to me. One of the most famous journalists in Europe had picked me to spend time with out of all the women around."

"That's because there's never been another woman like you, Giannina."

"Naturally not. They didn't have the advantage of being related to the man you were hunting. *I* was the chosen one and told you everything about myself and my family while you wined and dined information out of me." Her eyes blazed. "How can you deny that you used me in the cruelest of ways?"

A groan escaped his lips. "I deny it before God!"

She looked away from him.

"I had a young teenage crush on you years before we met again in London. I knew after our first evening together that I'd fallen irrevocably in love with you. Nothing else mattered to me during the month we were together. That was the happiest time of my life."

She shook her head. "You were so happy, you suddenly left London without telling me your secret. You didn't *trust* me or grant me even a half hour of your time before saying goodbye to me. You insult my intelligence to suggest you ever loved me. Loving someone means *total* trust."

He could see her body shaking. "I agree, but in our case I was terrified to take you with me in case you got killed because of me. If that had happened..." He couldn't finish his thoughts.

"I never saw you for three years," she accused him in pain. "Then two days ago you ventured into my office with my charming managing editor, who was already smitten."

He moved closer to her. "The postcards I sent were—"

"An affront to me!" she broke in on him. "How dare you mention them. You didn't even trust me enough to give me a PO box on the card where I could write back to you. How could that have endangered my life? Couldn't anyone have found them and killed me at the office?"

"But nothing happened to either of us in London. Once you'd gone back to Salonica, no one ever saw me with you again, so your life wasn't in danger. The postcards were my only way to let you know that you were constantly in my heart."

Caustic laughter escaped. "And when you did come to Greece a few days ago, it—"

"It was to protect you and your family before the news came out about your uncle. I wanted you to be there when he was arrested so you'd see the truth of his malevolence for yourself."

He heard a harsh intake of breath. "Please let's not do this, Philip."

"I'm in love with you and always have been. You charmed me as a girl. When we met up again in England, the reality of your beauty and intelligence overpowered me and I've never been the same."

She refused to look at him. "You didn't even make love to me."

"I didn't dare take the risk of getting you pregnant while we were in London. Furthermore, I wanted you to be my wife before I took you to bed for the first time. You're the only woman I'll ever love and want to marry."

Her head reared, causing her shiny hair to flounce. “Well, I have news for you. The man *I* want to marry doesn’t exist yet. Maybe never. When or if he ever makes an appearance, he’ll trust me with all his heart, might, mind and soul.”

“I already do,” he fought back. “Asking you to be my bride means you’ll be my lover and wife, the mother of our children. If I’m put on the throne, you’ll be queen of Hellenia, beloved by everyone.”

“Queen?” She stared at him as if he were insane. “That’s the last thing on earth I would ever want to be.”

“Why do you say that?”

“I can’t imagine being a royal.” Her words pierced him. “If you’d told me the truth in London, I would have checked myself out of school and flown home that very day.”

“Giannina—”

“Please leave.”

She was too hurt and angry for him to try to reason with her right now. “I’ll go, but I'm not giving up on us. We love each other and we'll find a way."

It was two in the morning as he left her apartment knowing there'd be no sleep for him now. He raced down the hall to the back stairs. Once outside he headed for the swimming pool at the side of the palace. A workout would exhaust him.

But as he found out after reaching his room two hours later, no activity helped relieve his pain. While he was changing clothes, a new fear gripped him. He'd lied to her in the worst possible way a man could hurt the woman he loved, but she wasn't the kind of person who went into hysterics. Instead she would find a way to slip out of the palace without telling him and leave for Salonica.

If he phoned or texted her, she wouldn't answer. With pounding heart, Alex changed clothes and hurried to her apartment. He checked his watch. Quarter to five. He knocked on her door, but there was no answer.

"Giannina? Are you awake?"

He waited. Still no answer. Hoping she would forgive him, he opened the door, but didn't go in. "If you can hear me, let me know. I have to talk to you."

The quiet alarmed him. Something told him she'd gone.

After dashing back to his room for his wallet and keys, he raced out the door and down the staircase to the foyer. One of the night staff approached him. "Your Highness? I was told by Kyria Angelis to tell you goodbye. She called for a taxi."

He could hardly breathe. "How long ago did she leave?"

"It has been half an hour."

Maybe there was still time to catch up with her. "Thank you, Jakov. Please tell Uncle Zikos I've gone after her and will be in touch with him."

Alex pulled out his phone and asked Ivan to drive around to the entrance to the palace. He needed to leave for the airport immediately.

If she'd phoned her brother to send the Angelis jet, it was possible he might miss her. Then again maybe she didn't want to bother him and had decided to fly commercial. Alex's instinct told him the latter was what she'd done.

He stepped outside to wait for Ivan, who arrived in record time. They left for the airport. En route he phoned the pilot to be ready to fly him to Salonica. When they reached the main terminal, Alex told Ivan to wait and rushed inside. The place was packed with tourists.

There was no sign of Giannina. He hurried to the gate for the flight and found her seated while she waited to board. Relieved to realize she hadn't left yet, he walked over to her. She'd dressed in a small black-on-white print sundress and jacket with white sandals to match. He loved her hair cascading to her shoulders. Alex could eat her alive.

When she saw him, she got up from the chair with her overnight bag and walked away to avoid people. "Don't try to stop me," she whispered.

"I swear I wouldn't do that," he spoke softly after catching up to her. "But I brought you to Croatia and I would like to take you back to Salonica. We'll fly there together in my uncle's jet. It will give us the time we need to finish talking."

"There's nothing more to say." She kept her voice low.

"If it's because you don't want to be married to a ruling prince, then I won't accept the throne. You're the most important person in my life. I'll do whatever is necessary to have you for my wife and live a normal life with you."

CHAPTER SIX

GIANNINA COULDN'T BELIEVE what she'd just heard. After a grateful nation wanted to crown him king, he'd give it up for *her*? Her heart was exploding in her chest.

Here they were in a busy airport terminal and Philip had just walked up to her with a declaration that almost made her legs buckle. He *was* the crown prince of Hellenia. She knew in her soul that after all the agony he'd been through over the years, he wouldn't say something like that to her if he didn't mean it.

One glance at the pain coming from those gorgeous black eyes revealed he'd been suffering after telling her the reason for his lie. Admittedly it had taken uncommon courage, as Nico had said.

How could she insist that she never

wanted to see him again and just fly away when yesterday she'd cried out her love for him? She at least needed to hear him out before everything ended. Once they landed in Salonica, he would drive her to her apartment. Giannina couldn't think beyond that point.

"I'll come," she murmured and started walking toward the entrance to the terminal. He reached it before she did and opened the doors for her. The black sedan stood waiting in a lane close by. She got in the back without his help. Alex gave Ivan instructions and slid in next to her.

They reached the small airport and climbed on board the jet. Giannina strapped herself in and left a text for her brother that she was returning to Salonica. Without telling him what had happened, she said she would have news for him after she landed. He texted back that he'd meet her at the apartment later.

When they'd achieved cruising speed, the steward brought them a meal with hot coffee, fortifying her. It tasted good. Her chaotic emotions had sapped her of strength, and she realized she needed sustenance.

"We'll be landing soon," Alex spoke after devouring his food. "But I need to ask you a favor. Zikos just texted me that he's convening an emergency session of parliament in Loria. He doesn't want anything leaked out about me yet. The plan is for me to lie low for the next twelve hours before I return to Hellenia. I'm assuming nothing will go wrong until I can join them, but better to be safe."

She shook her head. "You shouldn't have come after me at the airport."

"I'd do anything for you, Giannina. But my unmasking has caused complications. When I take you to your apartment, will you let me come in with you? Together we can enter your building through the back. People will assume I'm one of your boyfriends."

Her pulse raced off the charts. "Couldn't you go to your own apartment?"

"Someone on the staff there will question what I'm doing in the Dimas apartment. After years of planning for Hellenia to be a free country again, I can't allow anything to go wrong at the last moment. Zikos is depending on me to be careful."

She wanted to refuse him. But he'd risked exposure to come after her. When she thought of the consequences to everything he and Zikos Novak had been planning for his triumphant return to Hellenia, she found she couldn't deny him.

"Just for tonight," she warned him and felt his black gaze burn through her. "I hope you understand that nothing has been resolved between us."

"I'm aware of that. I also know I don't deserve your help. Perhaps now you realize that there's not another woman on earth to match you. I adore you, my love."

The fasten-seat-belts sign went on. They were descending. After the landing, she undid hers and got up to leave the jet. He carried her overnight bag and before long they reached the parking area, where he helped her into his rental car.

Early evening had come to Salonica. Three years ago, she would have given anything to bring Philip home to her apartment. *Stop it. Philip Dimas doesn't exist. In his place is the prince of Hellenia, a man I don't know.*

He drove to her apartment and pulled around the back to park along the access road. They both undid their seat belts. "I see a night watchman near the back entrance."

"He's always there," she murmured.

In the next breath, he put his arm around her and pulled her close. "Let's make this real, shall we?" he spoke against her lips before covering her mouth with his own.

The action was so unexpected, it caught her off guard. She found herself responding to the hunger of his kiss. It grew longer and deeper until she forgot everything but her need of him. He took her back to those evenings in London where they'd gone on long walks and embraced, not able to get enough of each other. Right now, he caressed every inch of her face before his mouth plundered hers again.

"It's been too long, Giannina." She couldn't tell if the moans came from her or from both of them. They weren't close enough. He molded her against him, kissing her neck and hair until she trembled with desire.

Suddenly she realized where this was leading, where she *wanted* it to lead. White-hot heat suffused her face to think she'd lost control and he knew it. She pulled away from him, struggling for breath. "I would imagine we've convinced the night watchman."

A knowing smile appeared on Alex's lips. "Plus the security guards Zikos has sent to guard me."

"They'll be guarding you from now," Giannina murmured. "You're the prince." His whole life had changed.

He got out his side of the car and came around to help her. She reached for her key while he retrieved her bag and one of his from the trunk. Carrying both with one arm, he put his other arm around her shoulders and nibbled the side of her neck as they hurried past the man.

Once she'd unlocked the door, they entered the building. Thankfully no one was around, and they took the elevator to her three-bedroom apartment. After she unlocked the door, he swept them inside. Putting down the bags, he cupped her face in his hands. A light shone from the recesses of those fiery black eyes. "Thanks to you, we've made it in safely."

He lowered his head and kissed her mouth again, as if planning to take up where they'd left off. Fighting for her sanity, she wheeled away from him and carried her bag to the bedroom. While she freshened up, she discovered herself more out of breath than ever.

Once she'd gotten a grip on her emotions, she walked into the living room. Naturally she found him on the phone speaking Croatian while he drank a cola. She sat down on the couch where she'd left her purse and waited for him to hang up.

Her friends would call him the hunk of hunks. When the news came out with his photo, every woman young or old would stop in their tracks and figure out a way to meet the tall, dark, dashing prince of Hellenia.

Giannina had just been thoroughly kissed by him and still felt the upheaval inside her body. Too many unsatisfied longings cried out for the kind of satisfaction she knew only he could give, but he wouldn't let that happen until she became his wife.

A few minutes later she heard Nico's familiar knock on the door. Alex darted her a questioning glance before he went in one of the bedrooms and shut the door.

She hurried across the room to let him in. Her handsome brother rushed inside. "You're home and safe." He hugged her hard. *"Echaristó parádeiso."*

"Thank heaven is right." Giannina kissed his cheek. "And someone else is here with me."

His brows lifted in surprise. "You're talking about Philip?"

She bit her lip. "Actually no." Her heart pounded too hard.

He stared at her from those intelligent dark eyes. "Then who?"

"The prince of Hellenia is in the middle bedroom on the phone."

Nico gripped her arms. "The prince. He's really here?"

"Yes."

"I saw no security."

"He assured me it's there. Why don't I knock on the door and let him know it's okay to come out."

"Wait—where's Philip?"

She took another breath. "That's a long story. The prince will explain."

He frowned. "You're being very mysterious."

"That's my fault."

Another deep male voice reverberated in the living room. They both turned as Alex walked toward them, bigger than life. Every time she looked at him, she could hardly breathe.

"You have to be Nico Angelis, Kyria Angelis's brother. Your fame is legendary, and I'd recognize you anywhere."

She looked searchingly at Nico. "May I introduce you to Prince Alexandros of Hellenia, *formerly* known to the world as Philip Dimas."

Her brother was a quick study. As comprehension dawned, he stared hard at her before letting out a long whistle. Turning to the prince, he said, "This is an incredible moment for me, Your Highness." The two men shook hands and took their measure of each other.

"For me too." Alex smiled. "I've waited fourteen years for this day. General Ruiz has been arrested and every Hellenian will taste freedom again."

Nico had been given a lot to process and

his expression sobered. "It grieves me and Giannina that our uncle was one of the men responsible for the deaths of your parents. What we can say with joy is that the prince of Hellenia will finally serve as the country's new king. It's a great honor to meet you. If there's anything we can do to help, you have only to ask."

Alex's penetrating gaze focused on her. "Your sister has been kind and brave enough to let me hide here tonight. There are reasons I don't want to be seen until my uncle has met with the parliament and they're informed about me. It's happening now, but we'll have to see. If there's a delay, I'll make other plans to stay hidden."

Nico frowned. "That would present a definite problem. It would be better and safer to stay completely out of sight away from the city where your privacy is guaranteed. If you would permit, I'll drive you and Giannina to my office building now."

Giannina wondered what in heaven's name her brother was up to.

"From there we'll fly in my helicopter to my villa overlooking Sarti Beach, where you'll have the best security available. You can stay there for as long as needed and have everything at your disposal until you're ready to get back to Hellenia."

While her heart raced, Alex eyed her brother with genuine warmth. "That's a very generous offer, one I accept on behalf of my nation with the deepest gratitude, Kyrie Angelis."

"Call me Nico."

"I will if you'll call me Alex."

"Agreed."

No, no, no, Giannina cried inwardly. "I don't need to leave Salonica, Nico."

"I'm afraid you do. News has leaked that our uncle is in custody for his crimes. There could be repercussions against our family since he worked at the newspaper all those years."

Her brows furrowed. "Of course."

"It would be better to avoid any unpleasantness until the prince's return is made public."

"Your brother is right, Giannina."

Nico kissed her cheek. "Since the newspaper staff can't explain your absence at this particular time and they're starting to get phone calls about Ari, it's best you stay away a little longer for both your sakes."

Giannina understood his reasoning, but she had other fears. After those soul-destroying kisses Alex had given her out in the car, she'd been shaken all over again by needs she couldn't seem to control.

He wanted to marry her and said he would give up the throne for her. But could he really do that? What kind of a queen would she make? What if he grew disappointed in her and in time his duties took precedence over her? Or worse, what if he gave up the crown and then regretted it bitterly. She wasn't at all sure she could marry him under such circumstances. She had to make him understand.

While she struggled with her fears, Nico

reached in his pocket for his phone. “I’ll alert the security guard at my office and let the pilot know that we’re on our way.”

Alex had already pulled out his cell. “I’m letting Zikos know what’s happened. He’ll keep my bodyguards informed. One of them will drive the rental car back to my apartment.”

While history was taking place, Giannina walked to her bedroom for the overnight bag she hadn’t yet unpacked. Alex had accepted Nico’s genius plan to get them away from the city. She knew her brother was devastated over what their uncle Ari had done to the royal family and wanted to do anything he could for the prince.

Earlier this evening she’d believed Alex would leave in the morning and get back to Hellenia. Once gone, she would never have to see him again except in the news. Nothing ever turned out as she thought.

The setting of Nico’s villa represented a paradise she’d wanted to show him three years ago. She’d dreamed of being there and lying in his arms, but his deception had ended those fantasies. Her only hope rested in Nico. She would prevail on him to stay with them until he felt it was safe for her to fly back to Salonica.

After a short flight to Sithonia, the helicopter landed at the back of the Angelis villa in the middle of the night. Alex had traveled to the Halkidiki Peninsula on several occasions and loved the scenery. This isolated spot overlooking the sea couldn't have provided a more perfect place for him to stay out of the public eye.

He'd found a powerful ally in Gianinna's protective brother, who'd insisted she come with them. Though the man had every right to feel hostile toward Alex over his lie of omission to Giannina, he'd encouraged her to go to Mount Athos with Alex to witness Hatzi's downfall. Now he'd offered him his home for an indefinite period.

Nothing could have made Alex happier. He needed time to try to win her over and

Nico Angelis was the only person who could help make that happen.

Giannina had sat in the back with him during the flight, but she hadn't participated in the conversation with him and Nico. Once they touched ground, Nico helped her out while Alex reached for their bags. He followed them down the path to the stunning white villa located in the greenery. Starlight illuminated it.

In the living room Nico introduced him to Thanos and Anna, the trusted older married couple who looked after the place. "Alex? These two will help you with whatever you want or need. Now I'm afraid I have to get back to home."

"You're leaving?" Giannina cried. Alex heard the anxiety in her voice.

"I promised Alexa I wouldn't stay. Nico has been fussy." He kissed her cheek. "Call me if there's anything else I can do. Alex? If an emergency should arise and you have to get to Hellenia, the helicopter will be at your disposal."

"I'm indebted to you, Nico. In return it will be my privilege to give Giannina my story to be announced in your family's newspaper. I can tell you with absolute authority she's the only person in this world I would trust with the truth."

Nico nodded. "She will never publish a greater story or set of headlines in this century."

The two men smiled at each other before Alex saw her catch hold of her brother's arm. "I'll walk you out."

When they had disappeared, the older woman said, "If you'll follow me, *kyrie*, I'll show you to your room and fix you a meal."

"That's very kind, but I ate earlier." He picked up his suitcase and they walked down a hallway into a guest bedroom that would have a glorious view of the sea by morning.

"The en suite bathroom has all the toiletries you will need. There's a robe hanging on the door. I made coffee in case you and Giannina want it."

"*Efcharisto*, Anna."

"*Parakalo, kyrie. Kalinikta.*"

As soon as she disappeared, he took a shower and shaved. This was heaven to be here alone with Giannina. But he still had to convince her of his love and gain her trust.

He put on a fresh shirt and pants, then walked down the hall past the living room to the kitchen. Overhead he heard the whirr of rotor blades. With Nico leaving, she would be coming back any second. His pulse sped up in anticipation.

Anna had prepared a tray with sugar and cream. He poured both of them a cup of coffee and took it into the dining room off the living room. While he waited, he reached for his phone and left a short message for Zikos.

I'm now with Giannina at the Angelis compound on Sarti Beach. All is well for the moment.

"Alex? I thought you would have gone to bed." Gianinna's eyes played over him, obviously noticing he'd had time to change.

He put the phone back in the pocket of his shirt. "Anna fixed us coffee."

"That was kind of her."

"Did I upset you by telling your brother I'd like you to publish my story? I should have approached you about it first. Forgive me."

She shook her head, causing gold highlights to shimmer among that profusion of brunette hair. "You're a famous journalist and the missing prince of Hellenia. If that's your decision, it will be a real coup for the paper. Every outlet in Europe, let alone the civilized world, would give anything for the privilege."

"I always wanted you to be the one, but I'm aware I've broken your trust and might never get it back."

She clung to the back of one of the chairs. "Even so, our personal history is not important to a world waiting to hear your news. We'd better get started on it soon."

Giannina was a marvel. "Whenever it's good for you."

"Why don't we say after breakfast at nine. It shouldn't take us long."

He could tell she was trying to have as little to do with him as possible. Yet again the nerve throbbing wildly at her throat gave him hope. "I'll plan on nine."

"Once it's done, you'll be able to fly to Hellenia. As Nico told you, the helicopter is at your disposal to get you to the airport."

Except that Alex didn't plan to go anywhere yet. Zikos would be running the timetable for him. For all he knew, their next meeting might not take place in Loria for several days. Right now he needed to be here with the woman he would marry no matter how long it took for her to believe in him.

After taking a long drink of the steaming liquid, he darted her a glance. "Your brother is one of the most intelligent and generous men I've ever known. I can see why he's always been your rock."

"I've been blessed with a wonderful brother."

"I'm glad you've put him on a pedestal. He is probably part of the reason you haven't married yet. The men in your family would be impossible for another man to measure up to. I realize that *I* don't, not after deceiving you all this time.

"That deception was meant to keep you safe. It's my prayer that if you'll give me time to show you who I really am, maybe a miracle will occur one day, and you'll agree to be my bride."

"Let's not talk about that right now." He thought he heard a little moan come out of her before she turned away from him. "I'm going to bed. If there's anything you need, just pick up the phone by the bed and Anna will answer."

"I'll do that. Sleep well, Giannina."

She rushed out of the dining room, putting distance between them. But he smiled because she would be only as far away as her phone. Once he'd finished his coffee, he turned off the kitchen light and went down the hallway to his bedroom. She was somewhere in the villa, but he hadn't asked her where she slept.

Before long he climbed under the covers, but his adrenaline would keep him awake for a while. Feeling adventurous, he picked up the cell phone and called her. She answered on the second ring.

"Alex?" She sounded anxious. "What's wrong?"

"Nothing that a little conversation with you won't cure."

A sound of frustration escaped. "So… after the coffee, you're wide awake."

He grinned. "Guilty as charged."

"In that case, let's do your story now. Give me a minute to get my tablet and we'll work on it. After we're through, you can sleep in. Tomorrow when you leave, I'll take a picture of you…maybe of you getting in the helicopter. Nothing posed, of course. I know you don't like that."

Giannina... Even though she pretended otherwise, he sensed in his gut she still loved him and there was no question she knew him better than any woman alive.

"The headline will read, 'Prince Alexandros of Hellenia comes out of hiding after fourteen years.' An action photo will make fascinating copy. What do you think?"

Why not? Except that he didn't plan to leave the villa anytime soon. "I love the way you think."

"Give me a second."

"I've got all the time in the world." Wishing she were right here wrapped against him, he turned on his side and waited.

"I'm back," she informed him, "and I've been thinking about what will be the most important thing for the readers. This will be the very first piece of news on you.

"Naturally hundreds of articles in papers and magazines, not to mention live television interviews, will follow. But this story will stand out forever in people's minds around the world, so it needs to capture the very essence of you from a young teen to a man."

His brilliant Giannina knew how to lay out a story and make it appeal. "What do you want to know first?"

"Some of my questions will be painful, Alex."

"I've lived with the pain for years."

"I'm so sorry."

Despite her anger, her compassion moved him. He had to clear his throat. "Go ahead."

"How soon after you were taken to safety did you know what happened to your parents?"

"Three men came into my bedroom at the palace around four in the morning, waking me from sleep. One of them was Zikos, who told me a tragedy had happened and I needed to go with them immediately. I had to leave in my pajamas. They hurried me out to a service truck at the back of the palace. In their haste, my dog, Achilles, had to be left behind."

"Oh, no! Your darling dog. How heartbreaking for you."

She really did understand since she'd played with his dog too. "To this day I don't know what happened to him. We drove to the port and left in a cruiser for Kavala, Greece, where we flew to Dubrovnik, Croatia, on a private plane.

"During the flight Zikos told me my parents had been stabbed and murdered in their beds. He assured me he'd made my father a promise. If anything happened to my family, he'd raise me as his own."

"Which he did!" she cried. Again he was thankful she'd met Zikos.

"He's a saint who had to endure putting up with me. I went through a difficult couple of years complete with counseling to help my depression."

"I can't even imagine it."

"I was in hell for a long time. My family had been so happy. The change from day to night turned me into a different person. I had no siblings, no living relatives. Through Zikos, plus a lot of help, I learned to live with my fear and face an uncertain future with new resolve to get on with my life."

Following his revelation, a long period of silence ensued. "I don't know how you lived through that. Thank heaven for Zikos." Her words touched his heart.

"Amen."

"I'm not going to print any of those details. Only that Zikos Novak, the closest friend to your father, took you to safety where he kept you hidden and raised you as if you were his son. From him you learned that your parents had been murdered and their killers were hunting for you.

"I won't say anything about your disguise or your identity as Philip Dimas. Until this day I'll indicate that you've lived with Zikos without mentioning the location. I'll say that he has been in touch with the parliament organized by your father and is standing ready to form a new government. How does that sound?"

"I told you in London you have all the right editorial instincts. It's perfect." *She* was perfect.

"Thank you," came her quiet response. "In a few words, will you tell me what your overall thought has been during these years of exile?"

"My mission has been to remove General Ruiz and his regime from power, thus avenging the murder of my parents and making Hellenia free once more."

"Is there anything else you want to add as a final thought?"

"That the goodness in a patriot like Zikos Novak always prevails and takes away the sting of a tyrant like General Ruiz and his ilk. I owe him everything, including my life."

Again it took her a minute to respond. "Do you want me to mention anything about your future?"

"Yes. That soon I plan to be married to

Giannina Angelis, the love of my life, *if* she'll say yes. There's a small summer-house in the woods behind the palace. I'm looking forward to secret picnics with her there and the dog we'll buy. If we're lucky, children will come."

"Dogs and children." She sounded amused. "How many are you imagining?"

"Maybe three or four."

"That many?"

He grinned. "I never had siblings and don't want that fate for our little princes and princesses."

"I think we're getting way off track."

"You're right. That would be putting the cart before the proverbial horse. I told you it's up to you if I accept the throne."

"That's not fair. I wouldn't want that responsibility, and now I think we're done. I'll run off the story and give it to you tomorrow to study and revise as necessary."

"Excellent. I'll see you at breakfast."

"I think we'd better make it lunch to give you time to sleep in."

Sleep was the last thing on his mind. "How about a swim in the ocean after we eat?"

"Do you have a swimming costume in your luggage?"

"If I don't, I'll wear a towel."

"Alex—"

Laughter poured out of him. He hung up before he said something that would embarrass her. Tomorrow couldn't come soon enough. He'd detected a slight thawing. Maybe she was breaking out of that layer of steel until she came running into his arms.

CHAPTER SEVEN

LAST NIGHT IT had felt good and right to have finished Alex's story. This morning she woke up still remembering a dream about a dog and a boat that made little sense. Remnants of her interview with Alex had obviously stayed with her. She feared the heartbreaking details he'd told her about that horrific night and early years would haunt her for a long time.

The fact that he'd known at fourteen he was being hunted by his parents' assassins caused her to ponder what he'd told her. He'd been so young and vulnerable. He'd survived a tragedy of epic proportions. On top of it, he realized he had a target on his back and evil men were looking for him. From that point on, Alex had been forced to get through his life and try to stay alive.

When he'd first tried to explain why he'd kept the truth from her, she'd been too angry and hurt over too many things and had refused to listen. But last night on the phone she finally understood why he couldn't reveal his true identity. He'd had to take on a totally different one. From the moment he'd met her in London, he'd wanted to protect her from being killed.

For the first time since he'd come to Salonica, she understood why he hadn't asked her to marry him in London. He hadn't yet found the people responsible for eliminating his family and knew his life was in constant danger. After his experience as a young teen, he hadn't dared put her in danger. That knowledge changed her entire perspective on his reason for secrecy.

Her thoughts expanded as she thought of his years as a journalist while he hunted for the men hunting him. She shuddered at the horror he'd been living through since being taken to safety, never to see his parents again.

She relived his story as she got in the shower and washed her hair. While it dried, she opened her bag and put on shorts and a blouse. Anna rang to let her know lunch was ready on the patio off the kitchen.

Giannina went to Nico's office and printed the story she'd written. With that accomplished she hurried through the villa to the patio. A hot sun blazed from a blue sky. Such fabulous summer weather should have put her in a vacation mood. But Alex's revelations last night weighed on her heart. To be constantly watching and waiting for something dreadful to happen wasn't a life she could comprehend.

She sat beneath the umbrella shading the table and looked over the story she'd written. So much she'd left out because the details were too private, yet he'd trusted her with the full story.

Since he hadn't come out to the patio yet, no doubt he was still asleep. Anna had poured lemonade for both of them. Giannina drank hers slowly while the older woman brought out fish salad and rolls for them. No sooner had she gone back to the kitchen than he suddenly appeared wearing a fresh shirt and swimming trunks. It took everything not to gasp. He had the build and features of an Adonis.

He sat down opposite her looking more rested than she'd ever seen him. His dazzling smile played havoc with her insides. "Good morning. You look good enough to eat."

She almost told him he did too. "Every woman enjoys hearing that. Have you heard from Zikos yet?"

"Yes. He's been meeting with members of the parliament who've been waiting for this day."

"It's a wonderful one, Alex. What a great moment for you and your country. It's finally happening."

His eyes held a new light. "Soon he'll phone for me to fly to Loria."

That meant he'd probably be leaving right away. She was happy for him. As for herself, she was a mass of emotions still needing to be examined. "I'm glad we did your story last night. Here it is to look over." Giannina handed it to him.

He drank his lemonade while he read. Eventually he said, "There's only one statement missing. After you insert it, I'll give it my seal of approval," he stated in his deep voice.

"I can't believe I left anything out."

He put down his empty glass. "It's the part where the prince plans to marry Giannina Angelis of Salonica as soon as possible."

She sucked in her breath. "Three years ago I was ready to marry Philip Dimas, the journalist who stole my heart. I'd have gone anywhere with him, done anything."

By now he'd tucked into the salad. "Will it help if I get into my disguise? I can do it in a half hour, and you'll have Philip back. Don't you know I'd do anything for you?"

She stopped eating, unable to swallow another bite. "How can you joke about a situation like this?"

His dark head reared. “It’s no joke. I’m deadly serious.”

“Alex—it isn’t your looks. Blond or black haired, you’re still the same person I fell in love with. I realize that now. But my problem is that you’re heir to the throne of Hellenia.”

He eyed her with intensity. “Before anything else, I want to be your husband and will do whatever it takes to live with you and have children. On the cruiser I asked you if you still loved me and you said you did. I’m asking you again. Knowing the truth, have you forgiven me enough to love me now?”

“Of course I love you, but that doesn’t mean I can see us married. Are you honestly saying you’d give up the throne to marry *me*? Don’t you know the world has been waiting for the favorite son to appear at last and take his rightful place at the head of the country?”

He wiped his mouth with a napkin. “But I don’t have to be king. What if that son would rather live his life with the woman he adores? What if all he wants is to make her happy?"

She blinked. "But you said that all these years, your whole purpose—"

"My whole purpose," he cut her off, "has been to avenge the death of my parents and make Hellenia free again from a tyrant like General Ruiz. The free government will choose a ruler from the people. I never said I wanted to be king, only that I hoped to work for the government alongside Zikos."

Giannina shook her head. "That's hard for me to believe."

"Why? When I met you in London, I fell hopelessly in love. So did you."

"I did," she cried, "but how could you imagine I'd ever be happy knowing you'd give up the throne for me? I'll never forget those news photos my aunt kept in the scrapbook of your family. You don't belong anywhere else. Your parents wouldn't want you to do anything but carry on their legacy and traditions."

His gaze fused with hers. "I don't know that and neither do you. I'm not sure if my father even liked being king. As far as I know he felt he had to do his duty, but that doesn't mean he was happy about it. Do you imagine I could be happy ruling the country without you at my side? I couldn't do it."

"Alex… You don't mean that." She looked shocked.

"But I do. While we were on the cruiser, I told you I planned to work in government. I could be a consultant for the new Hellenian monarchy. It would be a full-time job. We could find a villa there. The beauty of it would mean I'd be home in time for dinner every night with my wife and the children I want to have with you."

Heat filled her cheeks. "When we both know the palace is your home, you're not making sense."

"I'm trying to," he said earnestly. "Admit you'd love it if we bought a home in Salonica near *your* family. I could commute by helicopter from Loria. It's obvious you and your brother are close. You could go on being editor-in-chief of the newspaper if that's what you want. Or you could spend more time with your parents and aunt. I know your father isn't as well as he used to be. We'd make it work, darling."

"I can't see you as anything but a royal," she exclaimed.

"Are you saying you won't even try?"

She sat back in the chair. "I've read stories about royals who dared to live a separate life. I've always felt sorry for them. They've suffered for it in many ways because of their decision."

"I'm not one of them, Giannina. For that matter I don't have to work in government. Who knows where I'll end up if I follow my own destiny."

"Or maybe you'll become one of the greatest kings who ever lived," she blurted.

"That's a thought," he teased. "Come on. This glorious day is calling to me. Let's go down to the beach and enjoy each other. What would we have given to fly here for a weekend when we were in London? To have each other and this weather and beach is more than I could ever have asked for."

Troubled because his arguments were getting to her, winning her around, she pushed herself away from the table and stood up. "A swim sounds heavenly."

"Good. I'm glad we agree on that subject anyway." He got to his feet. "Let's hope you brought a bikini with you. I'd hate to have to throw you in the ocean and ruin those shorts."

How differently this day was going. "Aren't you waiting to hear from Zikos?"

"Always, but I'll take my phone with me. I'm counting to twenty. If you haven't returned from your room by then, ready to swim, I'm coming after you."

The gleam in those black eyes assured her he meant every word. She dashed inside and down the hall to her room. Her old blue bikini would have to do. She put it on and grabbed a beach towel from the cupboard.

"Eighteen," she heard him say as she hurried barefooted into the kitchen. “A wife who doesn’t keep her husband waiting. What a blessing you’re going to be!”

Giannina ignored him and ran down the steps to the road. It led to the beach. She could hear him coming behind her. The sand felt hot beneath her feet. She tossed her beach towel and plunged into the sublime blue water of the Aegean.

He caught up to her and pulled her against him. “Before we do anything else, I need this.”

The next thing she knew, he’d covered her mouth with his own, igniting her in ways she didn’t know were possible. The feel of his hands and mouth created such ecstasy, she forgot everything as white-hot heat consumed her. This was Philip and Alex all rolled into one, making her feel immortal.

They clung, not able to get enough of each other. She moaned when he eventually carried her back to the sand. After spreading the beach towel, he pulled her down and gathered her into his arms. Their legs entwined and he began devouring her.

"*Agapa mou,*" he cried over and over again. She hadn't heard those words for so long. Those were words she would have died to hear three years ago. "Will you marry me, Giannina? Tell me you love me and want to be my wife. Otherwise my life makes no sense."

She couldn't think. She loved both men, but one would be become king of Hellenia. It was an inescapable fact. He could pretend that it didn't matter, but the day would come when love for his country would take over all else.

Giannina knew in her heart of hearts he'd make a great king. But she couldn't imagine herself being his wife because the life of a royal was anathema to her. He needed a wife who would make a superb queen. The thought of Giannina being that person was laughable.

He was waiting for an answer. She had to give him one, but it wouldn't satisfy him.

On a groan, she tore her lips from his and got shakily to her feet. He stared up at her. "Where did you go?"

She sucked in her breath, trying to keep it. "Back to reality. I couldn't marry you and call you Mr. Pisistratus like any normal man who comes home from work at five. You wouldn't last five minutes, and I couldn't handle the guilt I'd feel that you'd given up the throne for me."

He got to his feet. His jaw had tautened. "You can't be positive about that."

"Yes. I can. I'm also positive that I could never marry you and be your queen. I'm not cut out to be a royal. It isn't in me, Alex. There's a certain logic in royals marrying each other. From birth they're taught their destiny and know what's expected."

"You're a remarkable woman who can handle anything and don't need to be afraid of anything."

"Except for one thing," she challenged him.

"Which is?"

"To hurt you."

His eyes had narrowed. "What in the hell are you talking about?"

"It's not what, but *who.* I've heard the tragic story of the fourteen-year-old boy who has had to make his way through this life carrying a weight no child should ever have to carry. By some miracle and Zikos's love, you've made it this far. So help me but I don't want to be the one person who brings any more sorrow to your heart and soul by being a disappointing queen."

She reached for the towel and started across the sand to the road.

Within seconds he gripped her hips and turned her around. "I refuse to lose you, Giannina," came the fierce avowal. "There's a third possibility in all this. The news isn't out to the public that the prince is alive. My existence can remain a secret. Life will go on in Hellenia with Zikos's guidance."

"It wouldn't work," she insisted.

"Of course it would. We'd be free to do what we wanted. You could resign from the newspaper. We could fly to a different country where no one knows us and get married. I have plenty of money so we could set up a business.

"Do you remember that we talked about how fun it would be to run a restaurant with the kinds of food we loved? We'd build a chalet that serves cheese fondue, the kind they make in Switzerland with Kirsch and gruyere cheese. We'd be the proprietors and even dress the part. It's the food for lovers and would be a total success."

"Stop, Alex," she begged him, not wanting to revisit that month in London where she'd loved him so much anything was possible. "You don't know what you're saying."

He gripped her arms. "I'm fighting for our lives and our love, Giannina. Can you understand that?" He shook her gently, then let go of her. "Maybe I've been wrong, and you have never felt the way I feel. I was so sure of your love, I believed we could overcome anything. I didn't know you could be this afraid." A haunted look crossed over his striking features before he turned and ran back in the ocean.

Giannina stood there devastated as she watched his powerful body swim out to open water. He was right. She *was* afraid.

So deep was her misery, she didn't realize that a phone had been ringing. *His* phone. For how long she didn't know. It came from his shirt pocket lying on the sand. She ran over and pulled it out, assuming it was Zikos, but the ringing had stopped.

She knew it had to be important and called out to Alex, waving her hands. When he didn't acknowledge her, she dropped the towel and ran in the water to catch up to him.

At some point he saw her and started swimming toward her. Within touching distance now, he pulled her against him and kissed her long and hard. "Giannina, darling. I need you more than life itself. Are you ready to tell me that you'll at least consider what I've said?"

He'd misunderstood her actions in swimming out to him. She pressed her hands against his chest. "I'm still thinking about everything, but I swam out here to tell you a phone call came through for you just now. I imagine it's an important one."

His face registered frustration before he released her and swam toward the beach. She tried to keep up with him. He raced for his phone and began speaking in Croatian.

She reached for the beach towel and waited for him. When he finally hung up, he grabbed his shirt and put it on.

"What's happened?"

He turned to her with a grim countenance. "Zikos returned to Croatia. I've been summoned there, but nothing has been settled between you and me. Now I have to leave. Zikos has sent a helicopter to take me to the airport, where the jet is waiting. It should be here within a few minutes."

Her heart lurched. She couldn't bear the reality of his leaving, but she couldn't tell him what he was desperate to hear. She loved and trusted him with all her heart and soul, but to be his queen…

The second Giannina stepped away from him, he strode swiftly toward the road leading to the villa. She hurried to catch up to him, but he was faster. When they entered the villa, he disappeared into the guest bedroom. Soon he came out with his suitcase wearing the same outfit he'd worn yesterday. The Alex who'd laid his heart at her feet moments ago was nowhere to be found.

"You're free to run the story in your paper anytime now. If you want a picture, better grab your camera. During the flight I'll call your brother to thank him for his hospitality and everything else he's done. It goes without saying that I owe you a great deal for your part in all of this."

She was in so much pain she could hardly function, yet she managed to run to her bedroom and pull the camera out of the case. At the same time, she heard a helicopter landing.

With no time to lose, Giannina flew out

the back of the villa to the pad. The helicopter seemed to float down, but the rotors kept going, creating a breeze. A man appeared in the opening and took the suitcase from Alex. They talked for a moment.

"Alex?" she called to him. He turned in time for her to snap his picture as he climbed inside. She kept taking shots until the door closed. Her heart plunged to the ground as the helicopter rose in the air.

Alex, Alex.

Dying inside, she raced back to the villa and phoned Nico.

"Giannina? How are things going?"

"Before I answer any questions, could you send the helicopter for me right now? Ask the pilot to take me directly to the newspaper."

"Of course. Hold on."

She didn't have to wait long before he came back on the line. "Where's Alex?"

"He just left on a helicopter his uncle Zikos sent for him."

"Finally Hellenia has a king again."

"Yes, Nico." Her voice shook. "I have his story and a picture. As soon as I get back to the office, I'll arrange for this to be the breaking news for tomorrow morning."

"It'll be the most amazing headline anywhere in the world."

"I know," she muttered.

"Hey—are you all right?"

"No, and I never will be again."

"Obviously something's wrong. I'll meet you at your office."

"You don't need to do that."

"I think I do. See you soon."

He hung up before she did. Since the helicopter would be here shortly, she rang Anna on the house phone to tell her Alex had gone and she would be leaving. She thanked the older woman for her help and hurried to the bedroom to pack her things.

The story she'd printed off lay on the kitchen counter. She'd keep it as a souvenir of her time with Alex and put it in her purse. When she heard the sound of the helicopter, she hurried out to the pad carrying her suitcase.

"Thanks for coming, Charon." She knew Nico's pilot well.

"Happy to oblige, Giannina." He made certain she was strapped in before they took off and headed back to Salonica.

"The boss says you have a deadline."

She nodded. "You'll read what it's all about when you see the newspaper in the morning."

He smiled. "Now you've got me real curious. Bad news, or good?"

"Good. The best there could be."

"It's about time."

"Agreed."

The short flight got her back to the city in time for her to say good-night to Khloe before she left for the night.

"Welcome home," her assistant cried. "I've missed you. Can't wait to hear what you've been doing."

"Come in my office and I'll give you a brief version."

"Whoa," Khloe cried out minutes later and rolled her eyes.

Giannina smiled. "Whoa is right. Now tell me how everything is around here."

She chuckled. "Chaotic as usual."

Giannina nodded. "Of course."

"I've left notes on your desk."

"Thank you. You're the best and deserve a bonus. I appreciate your taking over at a moment's notice. I'll see you tomorrow."

Once back at her desk, she called the guys putting out tomorrow's paper and asked them to come up to her office. When they arrived, she said, "You'll have to scrap the front page. We have a new one that takes precedence. I want the layout to be up style, with a noble feel that will stand the test of time. Don't let me down."

The guys stared at her in surprise.

"You're all sworn to secrecy until tomorrow morning when the paper comes out. I've downloaded the story and the picture that goes with it. This is so important it has to be perfect!"

No sooner had they left her office to get started than Nico swept inside. She jumped up to hug him. "Thank you for sending the helicopter. I don't know what I'd do without you." Her voice wobbled.

"Tell me what's wrong."

"Oh, Nico. That's such a loaded question."

"You're a newspaper woman. Just give me the nuts and bolts."

"It's complicated."

Alex flew to Dubrovnik to debrief. Zikos had arrived from Loria earlier in the day. The two of them talked into the night.

When morning came, Marko brought them breakfast and several copies of the *Halkidiki News.*

Alex sat there sipping his coffee while Zikos reached for one and read it. "This story was underplayed and an absolute masterpiece. So is the picture."

"All of it was Gianinna's idea. She wanted action."

"Her excellent taste tells me a great deal more about her. She'll make you an exceptional queen."

On that note Alex got up from the dining chair, so restless he couldn't sit still. "She doesn't want to be my queen."

Zikos's brows lifted. "But you've already asked her to marry you."

He threw his head back. "I did. She agreed to marry Philip but that man no longer exists."

Zikos lowered his head, no doubt disturbed by everything he'd told him.

"I'm sorry, son. You have to be in terrible pain. This is one time when I feel inadequate and am at a complete loss what to say to you."

Alex took a deep breath and turned to him. "The fact that you've always been here for me and are listening to me now makes me the luckiest of men. As for Giannina, I can't imagine loving another woman and will have to find a way to live with the pain."

He picked up the other copy of the newspaper and looked at the photo she'd taken as he'd climbed in the helicopter. Their conversation on the phone that night would stay with him forever.

Zikos stood up. "Now that the news is out, it'll be all over the media and we're going to be overrun with people. I suggest we pack and drive to the airport. From there we'll fly to Loria and take the royal helicopter directly to the palace. There's a whole staff and government officials loyal to your family waiting to welcome you home. They'll be overjoyed to see you back."

"You're right. Let's do it, Uncle."

Three hours later they landed on the pad to the east of the royal palace. Alex hadn't touched down on Hellenian soil for fourteen years. His emotions were running rampant when he saw a crowd of people waiting to greet him.

Some faces he recognized. The moment became surreal as he jumped down and was besieged with well-wishers shouting in Greek, "Long live Prince Alexandros!"

The hugging went on and on. On his way in to the palace, a man probably Alex's age drew his attention. "You probably don't remember me. I'm Evander, the gardener's son."

Alex nodded. "Of course I do. You and I used to play together."

The other man beamed. "On the day you disappeared, I saw your dog, Achilles, running around outside, barking. He couldn't find you and was upset. I took him home with me and kept him until he died nine years later. We became best friends, but he always looked for you."

For a moment Alex couldn't speak. He put a hand on Evander's shoulder. "You have no idea how grateful and relieved I am to hear this news. All these years I've missed him and wondered what happened to him. Are you a gardener too?"

"I still help my father."

"I remember you were an expert with cars and wanted to work on them one day."

He shook his head. "I've dreamed of working in a body shop, but the general wouldn't allow me to leave the estate."

Alex gritted his teeth. "Are you married?"

"Yes. We have a son."

"Lucky you. I'm indebted to you, Evander, and you'll be rewarded for what you've done."

"That's not important. When you're not busy, I'll be happy to show you where I buried Achilles. The general never knew what I did."

Alex fought not to break down. "Does your father still work here?"

"Yes."

"Then I'll seek him out and get word to you."

"Welcome home, Your Highness."

"Thank you, Evander." He hugged him extra hard. The loyal gardener's son had just given Alex an idea, one he wanted to discuss with Giannina if she would talk to him. “You’ve made this a homecoming I’ll never forget.”

CHAPTER EIGHT

GIANNINA WENT TO her parents' home the morning that the newspaper came out. They and her aunt Olga were overjoyed with the news that the prince had been found. Nico and his wife, Alexa, joined them. They brought her grandfather Gavril with them. He'd been a former diplomat for Greece who'd admired the royal family.

Throughout the day they talked about everything, turning it into a celebration, but Giannina was in pain the entire time. She wondered where Alex was now and what he was doing. For once, playing with little Nico didn't help. She envied her brother and his wife for being able to marry and produce such an adorable baby. Alex wanted a family and would make the most wonderful father.

Near the end of the evening she and Nico took their aunt aside and told her about Ari's involvement. Her brother had waited so he and Giannina could tell her together. They needed to do it now because of the leaks and wanted their aunt to hear the news first before the article was run. She handled it amazingly well knowing he'd been arrested.

She grasped their hands and said, "My love for Ari died years ago. He had a great flaw that grew worse with time. God will punish him. You don't have to worry about me. Thank you for telling me the truth."

At nine that night Giannina kissed everyone good-night and drove her car back to her apartment. After being with her loving family, the thought of Alex not being there was too much. Tears streamed down her face. She couldn't imagine how she would get through the rest of her life never seeing him again.

He'd suggested they find a new country and set up their lives there. Intoxicating as that sounded, she knew he'd been desperate to suggest anything so ludicrous. Giannina felt desperate too, and irrational. If she knew where to find him right now, she'd fly to him and beg him to make love to her. If she could lie in his arms forever, she would.

On her way up in the elevator, her cell rang. Alex? Her heart jumped as she pulled it out of her purse and checked the caller ID.

Nico.

She called him back immediately. "What's wrong?"

"That's what I need to ask you. I knew you weren't yourself today. Neither was Alex when he called me earlier. The man's crazy about you. I'm here if you want to talk about it."

"You're the best. He's asked me to marry him."

"But—"

"I—I wouldn't know how to be a queen."

"Does anyone? Chances are he doesn't

know how to be a king. If you love him, and I know you do, then be a good wife to him. That's what he wants, right? It'll help him be a good king."

"Oh, Nico. You make so much sense, I'm in awe." Her voice shook.

"I'm glad. I think you're making a mountain out of a mole hill. As I recall you had the same fear when Baba made you editor-in-chief."

"You're right. I was terrified."

"Yet it all worked out. Have faith in yourself, Giannina."

"I'll try."

The last time she'd been inside her apartment, Alex had come with her. She looked around, feeling an intense loneliness she'd never experienced before. He'd changed her to the point she didn't know herself anymore.

Needing noise, anything, she turned on the news in time to see a broadcast with the picture she'd taken of Alex leaving Nico's villa. "His Highness Prince Alexandros is back home today in Loria, Hellenia, after fourteen years of exile. The world is cheering the arrest of the ruthless General Ruiz, who put unbearable burdens on the Hellenian people.

"None of us will forget the brutal murders of the king and queen of Hellenia. Today we can all rejoice in the triumphant return of the prince. I, for one, eagerly await news from His Highness of his plans to restore a kingdom that has been ravaged by virtual civil war."

By now Giannina was in agony and turned it off. The whole world expected him to rule in the place of his father. For him to give that up to marry her because she didn't want to be queen sounded like…like the pout of an incorrigible, spoiled, silly, immature, stupid, out-of-control little girl without the sense she'd been born with.

For some reason she couldn't explain, she'd been destined to meet a man who'd turned out to become a king. It wasn't his fault or hers. They met and fell in love. It happened.

He could never be a government worker like he'd insisted he would do in order to make marriage palatable to her. His country wouldn't stand for it. No—if she wanted to be his wife, she would have to turn herself into a queen, for better or worse. But how did you do that?

Nico had told her to be a good wife and the rest would follow. But it still meant learning about a whole other world and how to act. It meant teaching any children they would have that they'd been given the most unusual role in life any child could have. What if their children didn't want a royal life and rebelled against it? What if she tried, but couldn't handle it? Her questions were endless.

There were other solutions. She could either remain single in life, or eventually marry a man who led an ordinary existence. Their children wouldn't be governed by royal rules. But that was the problem. So far, no man leading an ordinary existence had come along to sweep her off her feet.

Philip had been the only man who'd changed her world. Why couldn't Alex have remained Philip? His unmasking revealed another man who'd lived another life totally foreign to her. Alex had accused her of being afraid. He wasn't a superb journalist for nothing and had found her vulnerability.

She *was* afraid, *terrified* of not being all the things he needed.

An ordinary housewife had its many challenges, but to be his queen meant something else so entirely different… What if she failed him or somehow inhibited his ability to rule? What if she disappointed him and he would have to tolerate her? What if he fell out of love with her?

Giannina knew he admired her skill as a journalist and editor. But what if she couldn't measure up to his vision of how they would be together as rulers of his country? She'd been born a Greek citizen. Would his people accept her nationality?

She could apply for Hellenian citizenship, but would she always be viewed as an outsider?

When his country learned that her uncle had been one of the monsters who'd murdered their king and queen, would it change their feelings about the prince's choice of wife? Had Alex even thought about that? Would the parliament try to prevent their marriage? If they did marry, would they demand a dissolution of it in order for him to marry a suitable royal they could be proud of?

So many questions bombarded her until she sobbed into the pillow and drenched it. In this sorry state, her phone rang again. She wasn't up to conversation. The only thing to do was turn off her phone, but it was in her purse in the living room. She slid off the bed to get it, but almost fainted when she saw the name on the caller ID.

Her body trembled as she clicked on. "Alex?"

"Doxa to Theo," he cried in anxiety. "I

called your brother to thank him for everything. He told me you'd gone back to your apartment after leaving your parents' home. I was about to call my security people to find out why you didn't answer."

She sank down in the nearest chair, astounded that he'd even called and that he'd sounded so worried. "I had to hunt for my phone."

"Nico told me you've talked with your aunt about Ari Hatzi."

She gripped the phone tighter. "Yes. She took it amazingly well."

"For your sake I'm glad. Giannina—there's something I want to share with you, but it means you'll have to come to Loria. I know nothing's been resolved between us, but this is of vital importance to me."

She couldn't prevent the slight gasp that escaped.

"Tomorrow can you arrange to stay away from your office one more day? I'll send the helicopter to your office building to pick you up at ten. It will land at the side of the royal palace and I'll be there to meet you."

Giannina knew she wanted to be with him, and the urgency in his tone convinced her. "If it's that vital, I'll be ready."

"Wear something casual since we'll be outside most of the time. Sleep well."

As if she'd get any sleep after this phone call that had shaken her to the core. Once she heard the click, she hung up.

Wear something casual. She appreciated the suggestion since she'd feel like a fool showing up overdressed and wearing high heels in front of the staff. Being outside meant walking shoes. She had a favorite pair of khaki pants she would tone with a creamy-orange-and-white sleeveless top.

Toss and turn. That described her night. She awakened early and spent time getting ready. Hair, nails, makeup, including a pink lipstick. She left the apartment and walked to work to calm her nerves. After she reached the office, she grabbed a bite of food in the lunchroom before seeking out Khloe.

"Wow!" her assistant remarked. "You look fabulous. Where are you going?"

"I have a ten o'clock appointment and don't know when I'll be back. Would you mind taking over until I return?"

"This wouldn't have to do with that gorgeous Prince Alexandros would it? Until I saw his picture, I didn't think any man was better-looking that Philip Dimas." Her eyes gleamed.

Khloe, Khloe. "He's a hunk, all right."

"You knocked the newspaper out of the ball park with those headlines yesterday. The guys downstairs haven't stopped talking about it and the phone hasn't stopped ringing. I've dozens of calls from other newspapers to return."

"That's good, Khloe, and puts our paper on the map. The guys did a great job on the layout. Be sure to let them know there's a bonus for them and, of course, one for you. I couldn't get along without you."

"Aw, thanks, boss."

Giannina smiled. "Now I have to leave. Talk to you soon."

After years of planning for this day, Alex and Zikos had contractors already on-site for a complete renovation of the three-story palace. They'd arranged for the staff to live elsewhere and paid their salaries until they could return.

It was going to take time, but the result would be worth it. He hardly recognized it for the home he'd once lived in. The last thing he wanted was any evidence that the general had ever occupied it. He'd turned it into a third world compound that had been filled with his cronies and licentious living. Everywhere it reeked of smoke and had deteriorated beyond recognition.

Everything needed to be redone, including a demolition of his parents' spacious apartment at the rear of the palace on the first floor. But he had no idea what to do with that area.

Dressed in jeans and a T-shirt, Alex left the hotel in town where he and Zikos were staying. The large conference rooms could hold the parliament while they made future plans to get the country started again.

One of the first things he'd already done was have the huge spotlights, guard posts, barricades and electronic gates removed from around the palatial estate. He bought a car and drove to the woods at the rear of the estate, wanting to inspect the tiny summerhouse he'd told Giannina about.

By some miracle it hadn't been damaged, but everything else was a disaster.

As Alex walked around the palace surveying the changes he wanted made to the exterior and landscaping, he checked his watch. The helicopter should be arriving any minute.

There'd been little sleep for him last night. Giannina dominated every thought. If she'd changed her mind at the last second and had decided not to come…

It wasn't long until he heard sounds that

had him running toward the pad. When the helicopter landed, he opened the door without waiting for the rotors to stop.

"Alex—"

Giannina looked like a vision. He reached out to grip her waist and hugged her to him before lowering her to the ground. "I thought you'd never get here," he whispered into her hair. She'd worn it loose and flowing the way he loved it. "Welcome to Loria."

Her light brown gaze glanced all around. "What's going on?"

"As you can see, the general destroyed everything beautiful about my home, so it's undergoing a face-lift inside and out of gigantic proportions."

"Are you really safe here now?" She looked anxious.

"He's gone forever, and I have bodyguards on me day and night."

"Even so. How awful for you to have to come home to see this!"

"Don't worry. I knew I wouldn't recognize it, but that doesn't matter. It's in the right hands now and one day soon it will be restored to its former glory."

"Obviously you're not staying here."

"Zikos and I have made the Hotel Poseidon our temporary headquarters." He put his arm around her shoulders. "Come on. There's someone I want you to meet."

He led her to the other side of the palace where he found Evander waiting for him. "Giannina Angelis? Let me introduce you to an old friend, Evander Corso. His father was the head gardener in my father's time. He and I pretty well grew up together."

Her eyes glowed. "I was hoping you'd find a friend. How wonderful! It's so nice to meet you, Evander."

His friend stared at her in male admiration. Giannina was a great beauty and had never looked more breathtaking than this morning. "It's my pleasure, Kyria Angelis."

Alex pulled her closer, inhaling the sweet scent of her hair. "Evander has something to show me. Since it's a surprise, I wanted you to be with me."

"That sounds exciting."

"If both of you will follow me." Alex kept his arm around her as Evander led them along a path into the woods. Before long he slowed down. "This is the place."

She saw the two-foot-high white headstone at the same time Alex did. It was inscribed with the likeness of a Posavac hunting dog. The inscription read, "Here rests Achilles, the noble hound of his noble master, Prince Alexandros. He looks down from heaven, waiting to run with him again one day."

"Oh, Alex—"

Tears streamed down her cheeks. Before he knew it, she'd left him long enough to hug Evander. When she stepped away from him, she said, "This gift has to be Alex's greatest treasure. No man could ever have a better friend than you.

"I love you for doing this for him, Evander. I was only twelve when he disappeared, but

I'd been here a year earlier with my father. Alex and I ran around the grounds with him. I always wondered what happened to him."

"He was a special dog."

Her warmth and charm spoke to Alex's heart. Needing her more than ever, he pulled her against him. "Evander found my dog wandering around after I was taken away. He took the dog home and cared for him until he died nine years ago. I'll be indebted to you forever, Evander."

The other man blinked away his tears. "I loved Achilles too."

Alex had to clear his throat to talk. "This gift takes away any pain I felt at coming back to the palace. Thank you, my good friend."

"It's an honor to know you're going to be my king."

"We don't know what the future holds yet, Evander." He'd told Giannina he would work for the government and not be the king if that was what she wanted. Nothing was more important than to go through life with her.

"*I* do," Evander said in solemn voice. "Not all sons born to a king will make a good king, let alone a great one. That doesn't apply to you, Your Highness. We all loved you and have lived for the day when you would be found and wear the crown. Now I must leave you and go to work. It's been an honor, Kyria Angelis."

"And mine."

He walked away, leaving them alone. Giannina lifted her face to Alex. "When you told me you had something of vital importance to show me, I never dreamed anything could touch me more. You must be overwhelmed by what he's done for you. What a sweet man. Imagine having such a friend. I meant it when I said I love him for what he did."

"I love him too," Alex murmured. "And I've got a thought how to show him my appreciation."

She knelt in front of the monument to

trace the lines of the dog's head. "Is he a gardener too?"

Alex looked down at her. "Not from choice. He and his wife live with his father. The general refused to let him leave the compound. He's married with a child, but he always loved cars and wanted to work in a body shop."

"Maybe you could make it possible for him to get a job in town."

"That's a good idea. Before we do anything else, let's see about it now. After that, I want to take you on a tour of the palace and get your ideas for designing the interior. I'm starting from scratch."

She turned her head to glance at him. "My ideas?"

"You're a woman. I'd value any input you could give me. This is all new to me. But first, our errand."

He walked her along the path and out to his car. "I'm thinking we'll stop by a certain Realtor's office first. I noticed earlier he's still in business since my father's time. Maybe he's got some ideas."

The drive didn't take long. Alex pulled up in front and helped her out.

"Your Highness!" the older owner cried in surprise when they walked in together. It wasn't a surprise to Alex, whose pictures were all over the media since his story had come out. He was glad to see that no one else was around yet. "It *is* you, all grown up! What a great honor. We've waited and waited years for news of you."

"I've waited a long time too. Allow me to present Kyria Angelis."

"A great pleasure, *kyria*."

"Perhaps you can do me a special favor, but it has to remain a secret between the two of us. No one else."

"Anything, Your Highness. Anything! Please, both of you sit down."

"Thank you. There's a man, Evander Corso. He works with cars. In your business you get around and see things. Is there a body shop for sale?"

The Realtor looked through his listings and found three throughout the 2,200-square-mile island of Hellenia.

"Are any in Loria?"

"One." He nodded. "The owner is asking a steep price I fear he won't get."

Alex nodded. "What about houses for sale in that same area?"

The older man spread his hands. "How big?"

"Enough room for a family of four, maybe more." Alex turned to her. "I'm thinking he might want his father with him."

"That would be perfect, Alex."

"I will find what I can."

"Excellent." Alex got to his feet. "I want you to call him at this phone number." He'd written the number of Evander's father on a card. "I've also put my credit card number on there." In an aside to Giannina, he said, "My savings as Philip Dimas come in handy at a time like this."

Her response was an illuminating smile.

He turned to the Realtor. "When you can

arrange it, I'd like you to show him everything. If he likes what he sees, give him the keys and inform him the places are his. Put the bill on my card."

Giannina clutched his arm hard, giving him her approval.

"When he asks what's going on, tell him this is repayment for his care of my dog, Achilles. He'll understand. There's a big bonus in this for you too. Remember—this is between us."

While the Realtor stood there in a daze, they went out to the car and left for the palace. "It feels good to do something for a friend as exceptional as Evander."

"You've done something so marvelous, I'm close to speechless."

"I'm glad you were with me, Giannina." He loved her playing a part in everything. Life without her would be incomprehensible. "Now to tackle the palace."

"Do you want to re-create it in the original?"

"Not completely. I'd like to modernize to

some extent and make it even more comfortable, especially for children." *Our children, Giannina.*

Once they reached the palace, he gripped her hand and walked with her to one of the side entrances. Workmen filled the interior, but they stopped to stare at Giannina. No man alive could be immune to her feminine allure.

"Come this way." He led her down a hall to a huge extension at the back of the palace. "Let me warn you now. This was my parents' bedroom and suite."

She groaned and hugged his arm tighter. "I can't bear it."

"Neither can I. Something radical has to be done here."

After a minute she started walking, then spun around. "I know. Why don't you open it up and turn this whole area at the back of the palace into a memorial garden? Can their remains be transferred here?"

"Yes."

"Then do it! Visitors can come and pay

respect to your parents. The people never got the chance all those years ago. It would be a permanent way to honor them."

A memorial garden? Where did this marvelous woman come from?

He walked over and gripped her upper arms. "I knew I was inspired to ask you to fly here. You've solved my greatest concern and lifted that terrible weight from my heart. I love you, Giannina. You're the most precious person in my life. I can't live without you."

"I love you too," she cried, "but—"

"No *buts*, darling." Cupping her face in his hands, he lowered his head and kissed her luscious mouth, mindless of time and place. "I'm going to ask again. Will you marry me?" His mouth roved over her features, kissing her everywhere. "I promise we'll have a wonderful life. We need each other. You know we do."

She couldn't deny her need of him. She loved him heart, mind and soul, but she couldn't tell him yes. Not yet. Maybe never.

"Will you give me more time to think about it?" she questioned against his lips. "I can't think when you're holding and kissing me like this. You were born a prince and have planned for years what was expected of you. After the way Evander responded to you today, it's clear you're meant to rule. Give me a little more time."

"I will, because we love each other. Like any married couple, we'll make it work. Right now I want to show you the rest of the palace that will be our home once we're married."

CHAPTER NINE

IT WAS IMPOSSIBLE to refuse Alex and so she went on the tour with him. She couldn't believe the damage done by the cruel despot, but she saw the beauty in the bones of the neoclassic structure.

"My apartment is on the second floor." He grasped her hand as they made their way up the grand staircase. "This was my room."

French-pane bay windows looked out on a forest of deep green. Though most of the glass had been shattered and lay scattered on the floor, Giannina loved the design.

"Would you still like this to be your room?"

He stood behind her and wrapped his arms around her waist. "If you mean *our* room, I think we'd be very happy in here. I used to look out these windows for wildlife. A family of red deer would appear once in a while. I left fruit out for them."

She smiled. "Did they find it?"

He kissed her neck. "I'm sure they did because by the next day it had disappeared."

His stories delighted her.

"There are bedrooms on either side of this room for our children. One of them could be made into a nursery adjoining this one. On the third floor you'll find more bedrooms and what used to be a playroom, but I think you'd enjoy seeing the first floor."

He led her down the elegant staircase to the main rooms, where she found more men working.

"We had a music room with a grand piano and an impressive library. All the treasures, furniture, paintings and books were destroyed. Ruiz not only wanted to take over our country, he enjoyed destroying anything owned by the rich monarchists.

"He'd planned the assault on Hellenia for several years with my parents being the initial target. It came one night in a surprise attack that weakened security and virtually the nation."

Giannina shivered.

"The next thing I plan to do will be to organize our security in a way that such an attack can never happen again. The nation needs to feel safe before anything else. Without the proper policing and allies, chaos steps in every time."

Already he was on fire to establish his government. "History has proved as much. You have your work cut out, Alex."

A smile broke out on his handsome face. "But not today. I've wanted you here so you can see the kitchen and other parts of the palace. Then I'll want your feedback."

Incredible that he was talking about decorating a big palace, not an average home in the city. Taking hold of her hand, they continued the tour. So much would need to be done, but he didn't seem daunted. If anything, she found him energized. He hadn't been Europe's venerated journalist for nothing.

"There's one more thing to show you." He kissed her passionately before taking her out the front entrance.

She let out a cry of surprise. Forty steps the width of the palace leading up to the entrance filled her vision. Beyond them, a glimpse of the city of Loria. "How spectacular!"

"Walk down with me."

Excited, they descended together.

"Now turn around."

Giannina did his bidding. "Oh, Alex—" She was breathless from the sight of the exquisite yellow-and-white facade above. This was the only part of the palace that hadn't been ruined.

The second floor had an ornate balustrade that ran the width of the palace along with a colonnade. A fantastic ridge work with a taller centerpiece outlined the third floor and roof. "I've never seen anything so beautiful in my life."

"Neither have I." But he wasn't looking up. His eyes blazed like black fires as he stared at her. She felt their heat to the deepest recesses of her being before he gave her a kiss to die for.

When he finally relinquished her mouth, he said, "We've done enough for today and I've exhausted you. Let's get you back to the helicopter, but I won't make you climb these steps."

Before she knew what was happening, he picked her up like a bride and carried her up all forty to the entrance without being out of breath. "I've dreamed of doing this with my new wife."

She hid her face in his shoulder while Alex walked them past the workmen. He made for the side entrance that led to the helicopter. The copilot opened the door and helped her climb in the back. Alex followed and took the seat next to her. In a quick move he leaned over to kiss her and fasten her in.

"What are you doing?"

"Coming with you." He gave instructions to the pilot before strapping himself in. "A limo will be waiting for us at Salonica airport and we'll go out for dinner. I feel like celebrating with you as the man I really am."

She frowned. "You'll be mobbed, Alex."

"There's no time like this evening for a trial run. If you marry me, this will be our life from now on. Why not find out what it feels like?"

"But we're not married. Aren't you concerned about being seen with me? Think of all the unnecessary gossip it will generate."

"Giannina—I have news for you. No one will be looking at me. Every male out there will be wishing he could be with the most beautiful woman to come out of the Aegean."

Within seconds the helicopter was once again in motion and they rose in the air. "I wish you'd be serious. This isn't something to joke about and you know it."

He clasped her hand and squeezed it.

"I've asked you to come live with me as my wife forever. How can I be more serious than that? I know you're worried about being married to a royal. Have you considered that I might be worried about not measuring up to your expectations?"

The question brought her up short. She jerked her head toward him. "You couldn't be!"

"I'm only human, remember?"

She lowered her head. "You're braver than I am."

"I must be, otherwise I wouldn't have found the courage to propose to the famous beauty who ruined me for other women even as a young girl."

Warmth rushed into her face. "I was equally enamored by you, Alex."

He kissed the palm of her hand. "Why don't we take it one step at a time. This evening will be an experiment as a potential royal couple." Alex had the kind of confidence that made him exceptional. She needed to take Nico's advice and have faith in herself.

She looked out the window in time to see Salonica rush up to meet them. Soon they climbed down from the helicopter and got in the limo waiting for them. Giannina gripped his arm.

"I'm nervous to go out in public with you, Alex. By now, news about the general and my uncle is all over the media. Everyone will know that he helped murder your parents. Being seen with me could prevent the parliament from backing you. You mustn't do anything that could backfire on your dreams at this point."

His black brows furrowed. "You think I haven't considered all that long ago? The parliament will have to take me 'warts and all.' If they don't, then everything's off the table because I refuse to lose you."

On that note, he told the chauffeur to drive them to the Taverna Kaza, a restaurant near the White Tower with a live band.

"I've heard of it, but never been there."

"The concierge at my hotel recommended it to me. We can go dressed as we are. He said it's a favorite place for lovers who want to dance the night away."

That explained why she'd never eaten there. Philip had gotten in the way of every possible relationship. Because of that, Giannina hadn't wanted to be physically close to the men she'd occasionally dated.

"You look gorgeous." He pressed a kiss to her succulent lips. "We haven't been dancing for three years. I need this night with you."

Even on a Wednesday night, crowds filled the streets. It had been a long time since Alex had been able to relax and enjoy a summer night with his heart's desire. There was a festive feel with music coming from several establishments in the area.

He knew Giannina didn't want to be out with him where he could be recognized, but it was necessary. He'd thrown off the shackles of his disguise and she needed to see them function as a normal couple.

The restaurant with its potted flowers and trees had a certain charm. He'd reserved a table under his given name, but no HRH. Once inside, the host snapped his fingers to the waiter who took them to their table and handed them menus. The younger man couldn't take his eyes off Giannina.

"I thought he'd never leave," Alex said after he walked away. "The same thing happened when we went out to dinner in London. They'd line up to stare at you."

"I'm not listening to this." She studied the menu. "Everything looks good, but I'm in the mood for moussaka."

"That appeals to me too, and their best house wine."

The eager waiter soon came back to take their order, his eyes all over her. Alex could forgive him. The first time he'd seen her at his lecture, he'd probably looked as pathetic as the waiter.

"Alone at last," he muttered after the

younger man had gone. “Let’s dance. I need to feel your body against mine.”

Without giving her a chance to say they’d better not, he walked around the table and drew her out of the chair. Only a few couples were on the dance floor.

Alex pulled her into his arms. The touch of her, the brush of her elegant legs against his, electrified him. Maybe this wasn’t such a good idea after all. Once they ate, he wanted to go back to her apartment and love her into oblivion.

“Enjoying yourself?” He kissed her ear and neck.

“I’m trying to.”

“Surely you’re used to people looking at you. Men particularly.”

“Alex—I don’t like being stared at, but that isn’t what’s wrong. Don’t you understand that I’m worried?”

“That’s why I brought you here, to get used to the water.”

“I’m not talking about my first swim in the ocean.”

He chuckled and kissed her cheek. “In a way, that’s exactly what we’re doing. Taking a dip together where the world can see us. So far nothing disastrous has happened. If you noticed, our meal has arrived. I suggest we enjoy it while it’s hot, then I promise we’ll get back in the limo.”

“Thank goodness.”

He danced her off the floor and walked her to their table. Though he enjoyed the food and wine, Giannina struggled. Alex knew this was a new experience for her, but until now he hadn’t realized the depth of her fear at the thought of marrying a royal.

What better proof than to be out with her now and feel her wanting to leave the restaurant as soon as they could. Tonight had not turned out to be the celebration he’d hoped for.

Alex told the waiter they wouldn’t be ordering dessert. But after paying the bill, he escorted her back to the dance floor and pulled her into him. “I could do this all night. Just close your eyes and pretend we're the only two people on the planet."

"Don't I wish," she whispered against his jaw.

"Hold on to me and never let me go. I need you in my arms."

"I love being in them, Alex."

"But you still want to leave. We'll go." He kissed her quickly, then led her outside the taverna. They had to walk past dozens of people to reach the corner where the limo waited for them.

She hurriedly climbed in the back without his help. He slid in after her and closed the door, giving the chauffeur instructions to her apartment. Once they drove off, he felt the tension leave her body.

"I won't ask you if you had a good time, Giannina."

"I'm sure I ruined it for you. Forgive me for my behavior tonight."

He put his arm around her shoulders. "I forgive you anything. I love you. Our first swim together wasn't so bad."

She swung her head toward him. "I loved

being with you, and the Hellenians love you. But they're not going to forgive you for being seen with the niece of Ari Hatzi. It's ludicrous to imagine a marriage after what he did to your parents. Admit it!"

He put his head back with a sigh. "I agree this is something we'll have to wade through. But most people are forgiving and will realize you had nothing to do with the man who married your aunt. Give them time and they'll come around."

"I don't believe that."

Alex knew he wouldn't be winning this argument tonight. He told the driver to pull around the back of her apartment building. "I'm coming in with you to say goodnight."

"No, Alex. It would be better to end this now."

That was panic talking loud and clear. "In that case I want one last kiss."

He pulled her into his arms and fought for her mouth until she surrendered. Their passion took over. When neither of them could breathe, he lifted his mouth from hers.

"You know damn well this will never be over, but I'll let you go in alone this time." He reached across her and opened the door for her to get out. "I'm not going to tell you to sleep well since I know I won't. You'll be hearing from me shortly."

Giannina stared at him with a tormented expression. "For your own sake, you mustn't be seen with me. This has to be it." In the next instant, she got out of the car and hurried past the guard at the back entrance.

"Take me to the heliport," Alex told the driver.

By the time he'd arrived at the hotel in Loria, it was after midnight and too late to talk to Zikos. Tomorrow would come soon enough. For the rest of the night he would dream of Giannina.

At seven the next morning Alex rang for breakfast and called Zikos to let him know he was back.

"I'm glad you called. You have trouble."

"Bad?"

"Come to my room and we'll talk."

"I'll be right there."

When he entered the hotel room, he discovered Zikos at a table surrounded with half a dozen newspapers. They glanced at each other. "There's a photo I want to show you from one of the Greek tabloids. Naturally it made the front page and will be on television nonstop."

Alex took the newspaper from him and couldn't miss the picture of him and Giannina outside the entrance of the restaurant. The headline read:

> His Royal Highness Prince Alexandros enjoys Salonica's night life with Giannina Angelis, editor-in-chief of the *Halkidiki News*

Beneath the headline it went on to explain she was the niece of Ari Hatzi, the killer recently imprisoned for the murders of the king and queen of Hellenia committed fourteen years ago.

There was more, but he stopped reading.

Zikos looked up at him. "I've had a call

from the parliament spokesman wanting an explanation."

"So it has started." Alex wadded the paper in his hands.

"They don't know of your romantic involvement with her. When we've been so careful, it's understandable they want to hear details. A meeting with you is set up for a half hour from now in the hotel conference room."

Alex nodded. He needed to let Giannina know about the news in the tabloid before she heard it from anyone else. But he'd have to phone her after he'd met with them to get a temperature reading. "Any advice, Uncle?"

"Talk from the heart, my son. Be straightforward like you always are and see where it leads."

The time had come. Whatever happened, he and Giannina would never be separated.

"Good morning, boss."

"Thanks for holding down the fort, Khloe."

"Happy to oblige. Hey—you look exhausted."

"That's because I am." She hadn't slept last night and still didn't have the answer Alex wanted to hear.

Her assistant grinned. "I think I know the reason why."

Sometimes Khloe's needling could be a little exasperating. "What are you talking about?"

"This!" She handed her a copy of the *Thessalonika Sentinel*. "It came out this morning. You and the prince make one gorgeous couple."

Gianinna's mouth went dry before she reached for the local tabloid. After reading the whole story, she felt light-headed and dashed to her office to think. Last night he'd told her she'd be hearing from him, but so far he hadn't tried to get in touch with her or shown up at her apartment.

She could phone him now but changed her mind. The story in the tabloid had proved her point. Her mind was made up once and for all. Before the day was out, Alex needed to hear her answer to his proposal in person. A phone call wouldn't do.

Without hesitation she alerted the helicopter pilot she needed to fly to Loria immediately. After arranging for a rental car to meet her at the Loria heliport, she clutched her purse and dashed out of her office to Khloe's.

"I must leave on important business. Sorry to do this to you again, but I have no choice. Call my brother if something comes up you're worried about."

She eyed her curiously. "Sure, boss."

Giannina flew out the door to the elevator that took her to the roof, where the helicopter waited. The pilot opened the door for her.

"Thanks, Gus." She climbed in back and buckled up for the short flight to Loria.

The island country of Hellenia sparkled like a jewel in the deep blue water. From the air it had always resembled her idea of a dreamy secret land created by Zeus himself. But having seen the desecration of the palace firsthand, that picture had been ruined for her. Her stomach knotted when she contemplated how Alex must have felt after his return from exile.

Pleased that a car stood waiting for her at the Hellenia heliport, she drove into Loria and found the Hotel Poseidon on the car's GPS tracker. It was one of the huge hotels that attracted tourists from all over the world.

Alex had told her that under the general, Hellenia's economy had gone into a recession. But with the civil war over and Alex at the helm, she knew it would start to recover.

One of the men at the front desk smiled at her. "May I help you?"

"I hope so. I'm here to see Prince Alexandros. Would you ring his room to see if he's in?"

Surprise broke out on his face. He had every right to assume this was a joke. "May I tell him who's inquiring?"

"Kyria Angelis of the *Halkidiki News* in Salonica."

"Ah—one moment please." She waited while he rang the room. After a minute he hung up. "I'm sorry. There's no answer."

"Will you leave a message that I'm here and trying to reach him? Tell him I'll go to the palace to wait for him."

"Very good."

"Thank you."

In all probability he'd already gone there earlier that morning. Maybe she'd catch up to him. Since she hadn't eaten, she stopped at a drive-through for a *yeero*, then drove on.

Today when she reached the palace grounds, she noticed that all the barricades and gates had been removed. Thank heaven it no longer resembled an anarchist's compound.

The magnificent facade came into view. She slowed down. To think this had been Alex's home until that horrific night. Her heart sank before she drove around the perimeter to the rear and parked in an area near the woods. Lots of trucks and cars meant the workmen were busy inside. There didn't seem to be any sign of Alex.

He still hadn't tried to reach her. While she waited, she decided to go to the grave of Achilles. That might be the best place to say a final goodbye to Alex.

"Gentlemen?" Alex looked out at the thirty legislators assembled in the conference room. "To answer your questions about the tabloid reports that came out this morning, Giannina Angelis is the woman I'm going to marry. Zikos will attest we met three years ago in London when she was doing her journalism internship. I've been in love with her ever since."

A groundswell of murmuring ensued.

"I swear before God she had nothing to do with Ari Hatzi. There was no blood relationship. Her only sin was her connection to her beloved aunt, the sister of Estefen Angelis, the shipping magnate whom you all know. That poor woman suffered for being married to Hatzi, who used her abominably. Long before anyone knew he was a killer, she divorced him for his cruelty."

Silence filled the room. It could mean anything.

"The fact that the tabloid press printed this news so fast is a good thing. If you don't feel that the country can support me if I marry her, then I hope you find a suitable candidate soon, so you don't waste time putting Hellenia back together. That's the number one priority for all of us."

They nodded.

"Being a prince doesn't automatically make me a king. I love my country and will be happy to serve in any capacity you'll allow. Thank you."

Again, not a sound.

He and Zikos exchanged a quick glance before he left the conference room for his bedroom. Once inside, the red light on the house phone beckoned him.

Maybe it was their spokesman calling

to give him news one way or the other. A surge of adrenaline rushed through him. *"Nai?"*

"Your Highness? This is the front desk." His spirits plunged. "A Kyria Angelis came to the hotel to see you an hour ago."

With that news his heart slammed into his throat. *Giannina!* "Is she still here?"

"No. She left about a half hour ago for the palace but wanted you to call her."

Could his prayers have been answered where she was concerned? *"Efcharisto."*

He flew out of the hotel and drove to the palace over the speed limit. En route, Zikos phoned and told him the parliament council would vote and deliver their decision before the end of the day. He'd let him know the outcome.

Alex thanked him and explained that Giannina had flown to Loria. He was looking for her now and would get back to him later.

When he pulled around the rear of the estate, he saw a white rental car parked near the path leading into the woods. Before he explored there, he got out of his car and raced through the palace in case she'd decided to look around.

None of the workmen had seen her.

Now he knew where she'd gone…

Sure enough he found her sitting on the grass by the headstone with her head in her hands. She'd come dressed in a stunning white summer suit with dark blue trim. White sandals adorned her feet. The sun filtered down through the leaves, spotting her glorious brunette hair with steaks of gold.

He could see her body heaving though she made no sound. Alex absorbed what was going on inside her. So much sorrow revealed a level of pain that revealed the reason for her arrival in Loria.

She'd come to say goodbye.

"Giannina?"

At the sound of her name, she lifted her head, exposing a tear-drenched face.

"Don't get up." He sat down next to her. "The front desk told me you'd come by the hotel to talk to me. You could have phoned me from Salonica, but I have an idea why you didn't."

"What do you mean?"

"I saw that story in the *Sentinel* too. It appears your greatest nightmare has come true. We knew this was coming, but I'd hoped we'd have a few days' breather first."

"I told you it could happen," she cried.

"I know. Unfortunately a hungry journalist had to have been tipped off by a staff worker at the restaurant. All it took was one leak to set off an earthquake. No one knows better than I how that works. For eight years I made my living that way."

She avoided his gaze.

"While you were trying to reach me, members of the parliament met with me and Zikos at the hotel for an explanation of that tabloid story."

The news brought her to her feet. "What did you tell them?"

"That I've asked you to marry me."

"You didn't!" she blurted in despair. In

the next breath she walked a way off to get her emotions under control.

"I also explained that if they felt the people couldn't back me because of the family tie to your uncle, then they would have to find another Hellenian to run the country."

"Oh, Alex, no-o-o." She stood with her back toward him.

He got up and moved behind her. "Before I left the conference room, I offered my help for any job they'd like me to do."

Her body shivered. He saw and felt it. "I don't understand why you've done this."

Alex put his arms around her waist and pulled her against him. He buried his face in her hair. "Yes, you do. I've borne my soul to you. Ever since we met and fell in love, I've been able to handle anything believing that in the end we'd be together."

She shook her head. "It isn't too late to speak to them again. All you have to do is let them know we're not getting married."

"But we *are* because I'll never give up on you, Giannina. If I have to wait four, five or ten years for you, you're the woman I want."

"You're not listening to me, Alex! Uncle Ari's crimes can never be washed away for you. Your country has suffered so terribly for what he did. Do you honestly think they can forgive you for marrying me when I'll be a constant reminder of Ari? It doesn't matter that I didn't have anything to do with him. It's in their heads. They'll never let it go."

"Giannina," he murmured, running his hands up and down her arms. "If anyone has a right to hate him and never forgive him, I do. But it didn't stop me from loving you when I found out what he did. I'm depending on the parliament to understand the circumstances and feel the same way. Before evening I expect to hear what they've decided."

"I promise that they won't want you to have anything to do with me." Her voice shook.

He whirled her around, staring directly

into her eyes. "If that's the case, we'll leave the country as I suggested and start our life somewhere else. I could buy us a failing newspaper. With you as the editor, we could work together and make it great. I can't imagine life without you in it and know in my gut you feel the same way."

"Alex—you're not an ordinary person. Please don't pretend that you are."

"I've been Philip Dimas for fourteen years, an ordinary guy who got a journalism degree. It's the kind of work I know and am pretty good at."

She slid her soft hands against his cheeks. "Yet all this time Prince Alexandros has lived inside you, waiting to get out."

"*Agape mou*—don't you understand? He'll always be inside me, but it's not the sum total of who I am. Don't we want to have children? To watch them grow? Don't we want to experience everything in life? For so long we've been prevented from being together, but that's not the case now."

Alex couldn't take it any longer and

started to kiss her, molding her body to his. "You're my life, Giannina." He could feel his desire growing out of control. "I need to take you where no one will bother us."

She pulled away from him in desperation. "Zikos raised you from the age of fourteen. What does he say about everything? How is he advising you where I'm concerned?"

"Zikos isn't the kind of a man to interfere. He's never tried to influence me in my personal life. Why are you bringing him up?"

He heard her draw in a deep breath. "He's been your second father for years. Has he *ever* steered you wrong?"

"You know the answer to that."

"Do you value his opinion more than anyone else's?"

He cocked his head. "You know the answer to that too. What are you getting at?"

"That you ask him a straightforward question and wait until he gives you his honest answer. If he advises you against marrying me, which I know he will, then promise me you'll honor him and say a final goodbye to me."

His heartbeat tripled. He'd taken risks all his life. This was the biggest one.

"I promise, Giannina. But what if he surprises you and says he's very much in favor of us becoming man and wife no matter the vote of the parliament? Will you promise to honor him and marry me?"

What are you going to say now, my love?

"Do *you* promise? Say it."

She averted her eyes. "I promise." But she'd said it so quietly, he'd hardly heard her. "First we have to go to him together and listen to what he has to say, Alex."

"Agreed. He saved me and raised me like I was his son. I owe him my life. I love him."

"I love him too for loving you with such devotion. He faced mortal danger to get you far away from that monster and keep you safe."

He gripped her hand. "We'll go to the

hotel in my car and come back for yours later."

"I'd rather drive mine there now. It'll be a lot closer when I have to leave for the heliport."

She thought she'd be flying away in the next little while. He had news for her. "If that's what you want, then I'll follow you." No way would he let her out of his sight, let alone his life.

CHAPTER TEN

ALEX LED HER to her car and gave her a long, passionate kiss before shutting the door. Giannina trembled so hard, it was a miracle she could drive.

Zikos Novak would not be giving his blessing on a marriage to her. He'd consecrated his life for the good of the crown. In acting like a second father, he would make certain Alex followed in the footsteps of his deceased friend and king.

Once Alex knew how the man he loved truly felt about the situation, it would influence him enough to let go of his idea of being her husband. He'd promised her that.

Certain things in life were forbidden and unattainable. Thanks to Ari Hatzi, plus the fact that she was a nonroyal, their marriage headed the top of that particular list.

Giannina had fought him ever since he'd shown up in her office, so it made no sense she experienced a guilty thrill that he stayed right behind her all the way to the hotel. After they met with Zikos, she would have to put Alexandros Philip Dimas Cimon Pisistratus away for good.

One day down the road, she'd watch him on the news in all his splendor as the new king of Hellenia. It would kill Giannina to see the bride he chose. She'd already made up her mind that she wouldn't watch his coronation or his wedding.

In fact, she'd arrange to be on vacation when it came time for his nuptials. Maybe Canada. Her sister-in-law, Alexa, had lived in Ottawa for years. She'd urged Giannina to travel there with her and Nico to see her old haunts. That would be the perfect time to put thousands of miles between her and the man she would adore for the rest of her life.

When she turned into the hotel parking, she looked in the rearview mirror. Alex had stayed glued to her. Just the sight of him interfered with her breathing. He'd always had that effect on her.

She'd barely turned off the engine when he opened the door to help her out. But he kissed her first with an almost savage hunger that equaled hers.

"We can't do this out here," she gasped.

"We just did." He put his arm around her waist while they walked in the hotel. "I phoned Zikos on the way. He's been talking to some key members of the parliament in his room, so he'll meet us in mine."

"Did you tell him why I want to be there with you?"

"We didn't have the privacy to talk freely."

They took a private elevator away from the others that rose to the top floor. The doors opened on an elaborate foyer with chandelier. His apartment turned out to be the kind of suite reserved for heads of state or royals. He might like to pretend he was an ordinary person, but the rest of the world didn't view him that way and never would.

He lifted her hair to kiss the side of her

neck. "I'll get us something cold to drink while you freshen up. The bathroom is down that hall on the right."

"Thank you."

In a few minutes Zikos would be arriving. What he had to say would change Alex's world and hers. She'd always accused him of being the brave one. This afternoon she would have to put on the greatest performance of her life.

She brushed out her hair and applied fresh lipstick before going back to the elegant sitting room. Her heart jumped when she saw Zikos seated on one of the love seats holding a cola. Alex had brought one for them too.

"It's a pleasure to see you again, Giannina." Zikos got to his feet and came over to kiss her on both cheeks. It surprised her considering the circumstances. He hadn't done that the first time she'd met him.

"I feel the same way. When we left you the first time, I never had the opportunity to thank you in person for everything. I'm sorry."

He waved it off with his hand. "You were in a hurry. Alex tells me it's important that the two of you talk to me while you're still here in Loria."

Zikos didn't mince words.

She sat down on an upholstered chair opposite him. Alex handed her a drink and took his place on the couch.

"Before I ask Alex, tell me what's on your mind, Giannina."

His kindness should have put her at ease, but this was one time when she was jumping out of her skin with stark, cold fear.

"Alex has asked me to marry him and I've turned him down. There's no way this country will forgive him for taking a wife who's the niece of Ari Hatzi. Has the parliament already voted either way about his decision to marry me?"

"Yes."

His simple answer shook her to the foundations. "But you haven't told him the outcome yet."

"No."

That meant she'd been right, or Alex would already know. Fresh pain seized her. "Have they also voted about whether to allow him to be a part of the government, rather than be king?"

"That's correct."

"I see."

"I have one more question, Zikos. You've been his mentor since rescuing him from the palace that tragic night. He loves and reveres you. Your thoughts hold more weight for me than anyone else living. How do you feel about him giving up everything in order to take me to another continent where we can marry and live like ordinary people?"

Zikos sat there calmly. "Let me ask you some questions first. How do you like the idea of leaving everything both of you hold most dear in the hope of living ordinary lives elsewhere? Be careful before you answer."

"I don't need to be careful," she said without looking at Alex. "I already know the answer. It's the last thing I would want."

"And how do you feel about him helping shape the government without being their leader?"

She got to her feet. "It wouldn't work. Another leader wouldn't stand a chance with Alex being a part of parliament. Everyone already defers to him. Everyone's been waiting for him to ascend the throne." The memory of the look in the Realtor's eyes would always stand out in her mind.

"So *you* believe he should be king."

"I do. I believe it's his destiny."

"Do you think he'll make a good one?"

"Surely you're joking. He'll make a great one."

"How do you know this?"

She stared straight into Alex's burning black eyes. "Because of the way he treated Evander Corso at the palace on his first day back. Evander was his boyhood friend and took care of his dog after you rescued him. The love and kindness both men showed each other despite years of separation tells me everything about Alex's humanity.

That's the quality needed in an exceptional leader."

Zikos smiled at her and stood up. "Such eloquence. You, my dear, should run for parliament. If I've answered all your questions, I'll leave now. Certain matters of importance are waiting for me."

At this point she was frantic. "You haven't told us about the vote yet!"

"Didn't I?" He scratched his head. "They heard his defense of you and voted unanimously that you should be his queen. The coronation will take place after the palace has been renovated. It's their hope you will marry right away to bring joy to a nation that has suffered.

"That, of course, is my greatest hope, my dear. I never knew a man more in love and can see why. I beg of you to say yes so I can finally get a good night's sleep. It'll be the first one I've had in fourteen years, so have pity."

Giannina couldn't believe her ears.

What had he just said?

She stood there stupefied as he left the suite.

After the door closed, Alex wandered over to her with a new light shining from his eyes. He pulled something out of his pocket and reached for her left hand.

"You promised to marry me if he gave us his approval."

Still in a complete daze, she watched him slide a gold ring with a stunning solitaire diamond onto her ring finger. A perfect fit.

"I—I can't fathom that the parliament has given their consent," she stammered. "What did you say to them in my defense?"

"That your only sin was the connection to your beloved aunt, a woman who suffered anguish for being married to Hatzi and divorced him long before he committed murder."

"Alex—Alex—" She threw her arms around his neck and pressed her mouth and body to his, finally able to tell him what had been in her heart for so many years.

"I love you, my darling. I've loved you

since the day we ran around the palace grounds. I couldn't believe I was playing with a real prince. You were so much fun and made me laugh. When my father said we had to leave, I didn't want to go. After we returned to Salonica, I kept begging him to take me there with him again. He said he would the next time the king needed to talk to him. I waited and waited."

Alex crushed her to him. "I drove my parents crazy asking them to invite you and your father back to the palace. They told me you could come for my father's jubilee, but that day never came."

"Darling—" She buried her face against his shoulder. "I had a secret crush on you. Then Philip Dimas came to my high school to talk about current events, and I developed another crush. You can't imagine how excited I was when years later I learned you were giving a lecture in London."

He cradled her face in his hands. "I almost had a heart attack to realize you were the Giannina Angelis from my boyhood all grown up and so beautiful."

"I fell for you immediately, Alex. It surprised me how strong my feelings were right from that first moment. That's because underneath your disguise lived the prince, my young woman's fantasy of perfection. Don't you know my love for you is beyond comprehension? I want to be queen if it means I can be married to you. Nothing else matters."

"Agapitos," he murmured at the base of her throat. "You've made me the happiest man in existence. There's just one problem. I need to take you in the bedroom and not come out for weeks. But I want us to be married before I claim you body and soul. Since you heard Zikos say he would like our wedding to take place ASAP, I want it to be tomorrow."

"So do I." She half moaned the words against his marauding mouth.

"Then let's get in my car. I want to show you the church where I'd like us to be married and we'll arrange it with the priest. Shall we say three days from now?"

"What I'd give if that were possible."

"I'm not a king yet and can do what I want. Tonight we'll fly to Salonica. I want to ask your father for your hand and tell your family our news. Zikos is probably phoning his family right now. We'll keep it a small, private affair."

She hugged him harder. "I'm glad for that because I know things will be different for your coronation."

"That won't be for another month. Not until the palace is ready for us. In the meantime, we'll live here at the hotel. As for our wedding, I want you to plan it."

"I'm so happy, I feel like I'm going to burst."

"Now you know how I feel. Come on before I drag you in the other room and we retreat from the world for good."

That evening at the Angelis villa, Gianinna's mother pressed her hands to her mouth. "Three days?"

"I know it's fast, but neither of us can wait any longer. The only people we want to be there are our families."

"I guess being king, Alex can make the rules. That's kind of exciting. It's true you never got over spending time with the young prince. Your story is a true fairy tale."

"I know." Giannina giggled. "Of course, he hasn't been crowned yet."

Her mother caressed her cheek. "Just now you sounded like my little girl. Do you want to know a secret?"

"Always."

"Your father and I talked about it. He has told Alex to make use of the family yacht for your honeymoon. It will give you the privacy you need and keep you close to Hellenia in case something of importance happens."

"No one ever had better parents than you." She hugged her.

"Or a daughter as wonderful as you. I suffered when you came home brokenhearted from London."

"Little did we know Philip would turn out to be the lost prince."

"It's really incredible."

She nodded. "Do you think Baba will be up for the flight to Hellenia?"

"The doctor says he has improved since retiring. I can tell you now he wouldn't dream of missing the wedding of his precious Giannina. Olga is terribly excited. It goes without saying Nico is delighted. To think both of you suffered such heartache for years, and now look at you. He's never been so happy with Alexa and the baby. And you are *beaming*!"

"Oh, Mama. You'll never know how much I love him."

"That's how I feel about your father."

"Of course you do."

Three days later at the church in Loria

"Ooh—this white lace wedding dress is out of this world."

"Mama chose it. Thanks for helping me dress, Alexa. I'm so excited I'm shaking."

"I know the feeling. This is a beautiful church."

"Alex said it's where his family worshipped."

"What a lovely tradition. Nico and I got married at the church at Sarti Beach. He wanted to do it fast. No one knew anything about it since we didn't want to spoil wedding plans for Dimitra and Kristos. I think your husband-to-be has a lot in common with mine."

"They *are* alike in many ways. Handsome, brilliant, brave, adventurous."

"Keep going," Alexa teased her. "You've got it bad."

"I do. I'm so crazy about him I can't think straight."

"What's going to happen to your job at the newspaper?"

"We haven't talked about it yet. For now Khloe is handling everything just fine."

She handed Giannina her bouquet of white roses and stephanotis. "Is there anything else I can do for you before we leave the anteroom to join your father?"

"You've done more than enough. I love you."

"I love you too."

Alexa opened the door for her and they walked out to the vestibule of the small seventeenth-century church, famous for its frescoes. Giannina saw her father seated in his wheelchair. He'd been very handsome like Nico as a younger man. Age had made him more distinguished than ever.

His brown eyes lit up when he saw her. He held out his hand, which she grasped. "If ever there was a vision…"

"Baba…"

The organ music had started. He eyed her. "Ready to go seal your fate?"

"I've been waiting three years."

He chuckled. "Don't I know it."

One of the altar boys opened the doors and they proceeded down the aisle. Only a few chairs had been set up near the front to accommodate their families. She saw her tall, black-haired husband-to-be immediately. Though this was supposed to be an ordinary wedding, at the last minute she'd asked him to wear his royal dress blue uniform.

One day their children would pore over these pictures. When they saw how magnificent he was, they would burst with pride over their father. She felt overcome herself to realize this remarkable man loved her, had always loved her.

Zikos appeared resplendent as well in dark blue. He stood up for Alex. The only people missing were his beloved parents, but Giannina felt they had to be watching.

The priest came in a side door. He'd agreed to perform a very short afternoon ceremony in deference to her father and Alexa's grandfather, both of whom were in wheelchairs.

"Giannina and Alexandros, if you would approach and clasp hands."

Alexa took the bouquet and Zikos stepped back.

Warmth ran through Gianinna's body as

Alex took her hand in his. He rubbed his thumb over her palm in a private message that turned her insides to mush.

"Prince Alexandros?" the priest began. "This will be the last time I address you this way. God has sent you back to us a man, heaven be praised. May He bless this union.

"If you will repeat after me, I, Prince Alexandros Cimon Pisistratus, promise to love and cherish this woman through mortality and beyond, through sickness and in health. I will provide for her welfare and worship her with my body."

Giannina listened to Alex's deep voice repeat the words. Then it came her turn. "I, Giannina Panagos Angelis, promise to love and cherish this man through mortality and beyond, through sickness and in health. I will be his comfort and worship him with my body."

The priest smiled at them. "Bless you, my children. In the name of the Father, the Son and the Holy Spirit, I pronounce you husband and wife. You may kiss your bride."

The fire in Alex's eyes caused her to tremble as he gave her a husband's kiss she wanted to last forever.

"Let's go, my love."

They'd planned to forgo a celebration with family. That would come later after the coronation. Their ring ceremony would happen then too. He grasped her hand and they left the church. A limo stood waiting to take them to the yacht.

Giannina never remembered the drive to the port. The two of them forgot the world as they tried without success to show each other how they felt. Once on board in familiar surroundings, they went straight to the guest suite her father had picked out for them. It had windows overlooking the ocean.

Alex closed and locked the door before turning to her. He took off his suit jacket and tossed it on a chair. His gaze roved over her, not missing an inch, before he reached in her hair to remove her short veil. "Never has there been a more beautiful bride. I can't believe we're married and that I have you all to myself at last for as long as we live."

"I never dreamed this day would come," she whispered. "I still feel I'm dreaming."

He reached around to unfasten the back of her dress and slid it off her shoulders. While she stepped out of it, he disappeared into the bathroom. He came out a moment later wearing a robe and laid her dress on the love seat. In the next breath he picked her up in his arms and carried her over to the bed.

She clung to him as he lowered her to the mattress and began kissing the daylights out of her. Each sensual kiss grew longer, filling her with desire she'd never known. Wrapped in each other's arms had to be one of the greatest joys in life as they sought to give each other pleasure.

His hands and mouth brought an ecstasy she didn't know was possible. With their legs entangled, she'd never experienced such rapture and forgot the time, let alone her surroundings. Darkness filled the room before she had cognizance of anything but loving and being loved. Her lover had taken her to the heights and she never wanted him to stop.

"Alex?" She smoothed her hand over his chest. "I love you too much."

A deep male laugh came out of him. "Explain *too much*."

"If anything happened to you, I'd die. When I think—"

But his mouth stopped her there. "No thinking, my love. I've done too much of that over the last three years worrying about you, wondering what you were doing, what men you were attracted to, the ones you were kissing."

She rose up and half lay on him. "There's never been another man but you. A young prince captured my heart. It's been yours ever since."

"Darling—"

"I'm afraid you ruined me for all time, Alex."

"That day we played on the palace grounds sealed my fate too. You stole *my* heart and I never forgot you." He rolled her over and began kissing her again. "You've been my obsession and you haven't made it easy on me."

She covered his face with kisses. "I'm so sorry. You know I love you more than life."

"I'll forgive you if you'll order us some food. After it arrives, I'll tell you how you can make my pain go away."

She did his bidding, then put the phone receiver back and turned to him. "Just so you know, I wasn't too thrilled with those tiny epistles you sent that left no address or phone number."

"Those cards were a form of code."

"Code?"

"Yes." He kissed her earlobe. "You were supposed to read between the lines and know how I felt."

"Obviously they kind of worked because I'm now your wife."

"Indeed you are. In every possible way.

Do you know you remind me of the gorgeous Penelope who had many ardent suitors?"

"You mean the adored wife of Odysseus, king of Ithaca?"

"The very one. It's our story, Giannina. When he got back from the Trojan War, he was disguised as a beggar. She didn't recognize her husband or welcome him right away. It hurt him terribly. He had to prove to her that he was her husband so she'd take him back."

"I forget how long he was gone."

"Ten years."

"Well, that explains quite a lot, especially if he didn't write her any postcards at all. But as I recall, she forgave him in time, and they lived happily ever after."

"They couldn't be as happy as we are."

"No one could be," she whispered before kissing him again and again. Eventually a knock sounded.

"Our food is here. I'll get it."

"Just a minute, sweetheart. I told them

to leave it outside the door. I know you're hungry, but there's something I want to tell you first. I hope it will make you happy."

He looked down at her. "What is it?"

"Nico gave me some advice that I know is right. When I told him I was nervous about being queen, he told me that all I needed to do was be a good wife. The rest would follow. So I'm afraid you're stuck with a clingy wife who's so crazy about you, I'm going to be an embarrassment."

"Thank heaven!"

EPILOGUE

"THE NEWS IS very good," Alex announced to his cabinet assembled at the palace. "After a year, the economy has started to recover, and job growth has skyrocketed. We've opened trade relations with dozens of countries and tourism has risen three hundred percent."

Alex was gratified by the clapping and cheers coming from the government officials. They were responsible for the dramatic changes since the evil regime had been eradicated.

Zikos got to his feet. "You've left out the most important piece of news, Your Highness." He turned to the others. "In the first year of our new government, the king and queen have produced an heir, which ensures the continuation of the Pisistratus royal line. Hail to the king of Hellenia!"

The others sprang to their feet to offer their congratulations. Pleased as Alex was by their response, the mention of their five-week-old baby daughter put thoughts of the nation out of his mind. He flashed Zikos a private smile.

When the noise quieted down, Alex said, "I appreciate your continued support and enthusiasm. Thank you for your sacrifice to our country. Nothing could have happened without all of you pulling together. Now I'm afraid I have to be excused and help my wife do the really important work of the day."

As the room filled with good-natured laughter, he left the conference room through a back door and hurried down the hall to the grand staircase. Taking the steps two at a time, he raced up to their bedroom on the second floor.

There was no sign of Giannina or Zoe. Where would they be at four thirty in the afternoon?

He asked the guard in the hall if he'd seen her. "Yes, Your Highness. She said to tell you she was going out to the summerhouse and would wait for you there."

Excited about that, Alex went back to the bedroom to change out of his suit into casual clothes. Then he took off for the tiny summerhouse he'd had renovated.

Giannina said that the first time she saw it, she'd thought of it as the little house in the forest where Goldilocks met the three bears. He'd made certain it resembled the drawing in the book. They stole out there when they wanted to get away from the palace. Soon it would be a playhouse for their children.

When he walked in, he discovered both of them on the double bed in the corner next to a little table. Their precious Zoe with her brunette hair lay on her back sound asleep. No doubt Giannina had been nursing her, and now his exhausted wife had fallen into a light sleep too.

At the foot of the bed lay their dog, a replica of Achilles. The beautiful sight of the three of them touched his heart. Giannina had wanted to name him Neoptolemus after the son of Achilles. They called him Toly for short. The dog saw him come in and jumped off the bed to greet him. Alex hunkered down to play with him.

This was the kind of life with Giannina he'd dreamed of years ago. How long it could go on like this, no one knew, but he thanked God for this happiness and the most adorable wife imaginable.

Stealing across the room, he lay down on the bed. He curled his arm around her and pulled her close to him, careful not to disturb Zoe.

"I've been waiting for you to come," she whispered against his jaw. "I thought we'd have a celebration in here."

His heart thudded. "Celebration?"

"I had a checkup with the doctor earlier today. He's given me a clean bill of health, so..."

"But what about Zoe?"

She flashed him a beguiling smile. “Clista is outside to take care of the baby for a few hours. I asked her to bring the leash so she can take Toly with her.”

“Giannina—”

Her arms crept around his neck. “I wish parenthood could be an experience for every woman or man wanting a baby. But you need to know how much I’ve been dying to make love with you since she was born. She’s just been fed, and I can’t wait any longer.”

“Neither can I.”

He rolled off the bed and walked around to pick up his precious daughter. Toly followed him. A second later he opened the door to hand her to Clista.

“I’ll take care of both of them, Your Highness.”

“I know you will.”

Alex kissed his daughter’s cheek, fastened the leash to Toly’s collar, then closed the door and hurried back inside to his wife. She’d let her hair grow longer. It splayed on the pillow. She'd never looked more exquisite to him.

"Love me," she cried softly. "Your shameless wife is back."

"So is your shameless husband who couldn't leave the conference room fast enough to be with you."

"I'm so proud of you and all you've accomplished, darling."

He pulled her on top of him. "Zikos reminded them that our daughter is our greatest accomplishment."

"She is, so far… But who can say what this evening will bring?"

"I know one thing," he murmured against her lips. "You've made me the happiest man alive. Work your magic, Giannina."

* * * * *